Falling for You at Brew by Brewer

Pumpkin Patch Romance Collection

Elsie James

Published by Elsie James, 2023.

Table of Contents

Falling for You, Chapter One: Molly

"How's it going over here?" Isabela Brewer taps me on the shoulder and I look up from my clipboard.

"Fabulous. I so appreciate you letting us host our event at your pumpkin patch."

"Well it isn't exactly mine, but I know the whole Brewer family is happy to have you, it's for such a good cause. Let me know what you need. Hopefully, we'll raise a whole lot of money." Isabella nods.

"That's the plan."

On days like this, I'm reminded that I have the absolute best job in the world. I'm lucky enough to have made a career of finding funding for the Francis Hospital. Usually, the funds come through my grant writing endeavors, but once a year I get to hold an in-person event.

This year's three-day fundraising festival is extra special because we're holding it in my hometown of Misty Mountain at the Brew by Brewer resort's pumpkin patch. The place looks stunning.

Stacks of white pumpkins line the outdoor space near the barn with a stage in the center. The pumpkin patch itself is set up with livestock fencing encircling the large field, with gates and signage put up to block people from coming in anywhere that's not the designated entrance.

On top of that, they have everything fall has to offer in one place, a corn maze, hayrides, and a pumpkin launcher. Thankfully, we've had a steady stream of customers all day and the crowds continue to pour in. With any luck, we'll meet our goal.

When I was seventeen, I lost my only sister Holly to cancer. She was just twelve years old when she passed and I miss her every day. In the years leading up to her death, I spent so much time traveling with my family to and from Francis Hospital. Sleeping in the car. Chatting with nurses in waiting rooms. Having family dinners in the cafeteria. Giving back to the hospital means everything to me.

I'm on the platform stage checking off the last items on my list when a fire truck pulls up just outside of the gate. Isabella passes me, heading straight for it.

"What's going on? Is everything okay?" I call out to Isabella as I scamper to catch up with her.

Isabella circles back around to wait for me and her mouth pulls into a smirk. "I almost forgot to tell you. We invited the guys from the firehouse to come volunteer. It looks like we got quite the turnout."

My jaw falls open as I take in the magnificent sight in front of me. One man after the next climbs out. They are outfitted in black pants and navy blue t-shirts. Some have suspenders. All have mouthwatering muscles.

I haven't been back to my hometown in a long time but one thing I know for certain is that they just don't make men like this in the city. While Isabella rushes to greet them, I park myself right in the entrance and lean on the fence. I let myself gawk unabashedly. I figure it's the least I can do after all the work I've put into this event.

Firefighter after firefighter rush in past me. I study them as they fly by and sometimes even manage to let my eyes drift up to catch a glimpse of their faces. But one man, in particular, jumps out at me.

I squint into the sun. The eyes are familiar but the body is wrong. When he gets closer, I hear his deep, rich tone and there isn't any mistaking who he is.

"Taylor Henderson, what are you doing?" I shout with a laugh. His name practically rips out of my throat.

"What? I had no idea you were in town!" Taylor makes quick work of hopping the fence and he wraps me in a hug.

I haven't seen my old friend in so long, it's got to be nearly a decade. He's definitely filled out, his tall frame bulked with muscle, his jaw chiseled, and his dark hair wild. But at the same time, he looks like exactly the person he is, a good old mountain man, born and raised out on the back roads.

We went to high school together and every country song I've ever heard describes him perfectly. The Taylor I knew spent his weekends out fishing, went to the rodeo when it came to town, and followed bull riding the same way most people follow football. I'd bet money that none of that has changed.

"You're a firefighter now." I smile up at him then decide not to add, *also you're smoking hot now. Give a girl a warning before you hit me with all that smolder.*

"I am, my brothers and I came to the conclusion that helping people is for us." He gestures behind him.

I follow his line of sight. The familiar faces of his two younger brothers Patrick and Joshua come into focus. I've always liked the Henderson family, it doesn't surprise me that they would volunteer their time.

"We came to help raise money and it looks like the universe is already rewarding me for my good deed because here you are. You look beautiful. I think flannel might be your thing." His lazy charm is one of the things I've always loved about Taylor.

Although I know the compliment is just his way of interacting, it still makes butterflies flap in my stomach. "I can't wear it in the city but I thought I'd dig it out for the big three-day event."

I would have dated him back then, but I never had the chance. He dated a girl in our class named Christina since before I can remember. They married young. I never thought she treated him with the respect he deserved, but he always seemed happy enough.

"You're here in memory of your sister then?" Taylor asks and it's nice to be around someone who already knows my story.

"Well yes, and also because it's my event. I work for Francis Hospital now as a fundraiser and grant writer. But it's good to be back in Misty Mountain, even just for a few days."

"I always knew you'd do something amazing with your life. Look at you, big life in the big city. Holly would be proud." Hearing him speak my sister's name with such light regard makes me smile. He continues. "Let me guess, you and Bradley Beans have a high-rise condo in the city and he's got a job with a fancy title." Taylor rolls his eyes with mock annoyance.

"It's Bradley Lima." I can't help but giggle at the way he pronounces my ex-boyfriend's name with exaggerated emphasis. "He is a banker now. He loves his prestigious job in the city... and we actually aren't together anymore. We haven't been for a few years."

"You're kidding, was he too polished for you or.... He seems like the type to make you pump your own gas. Was that it?" His mouth curls into a smile as he teases me.

"No, thank you very much. He was a decent enough person, he just wasn't *my* person. It's sort of refreshing to know beyond a shadow of a doubt that we would never work. It freed up the space in my brain to move on."

"Tell me about it, there's nothing in the world that can be quite as bad as breaking up with the person whom you've tied not just your housing, but your car, your pets, and your whole universe to," Taylor says, rubbing a hand across the back of his neck.

"That's sweet of you to say, but how would you know? You've been practically married since we were just babies. I imagine you have that whole football team of babies you've always wanted by now." I laugh but Taylor doesn't join in.

My eyes flick to his left hand and I can't help but notice that he isn't wearing a ring.

"Well that's what I had mapped out for myself too but the best-laid plans don't always work out like you think they will. It's just me these days. Christina left me for her trainer. They ran away to make a new life on the coast. So after a year or so, I accepted that she wasn't coming back and we got divorced."

My mouth falls open in shock. "You're kidding. I'm so sorry to hear that."

"It's okay honestly. She's running wild and free and I want a small-town life. I'm content here and I can't imagine keeping someone else from finding their own happiness... I'm not going to lie, I could've done without the being-cheated-on part but..." He shrugs. "On the other hand, if I was still married, I don't know that I'd get to be here donating my time and talking to you. It seems worth it." Taylor winks and it sizzles through me.

I tuck a strand of blonde hair behind my ear and look away from him. "What do they have you doing today?"

"Sounds like I'm working the pumpkin launcher. It's that big ole slingshot thing over there. Probably a good fit for me. I can put these guns to use. That's the plan at least." He flexes his muscles with a dramatic chuckle and although I know he's kidding, my eyes widen.

"You know me, I love a plan. I'll be walking around with a clipboard checking things off my list if you need anything." I rub the sweat from my palms on the sides of my pants. I can't believe how nervous I am around Taylor now that I know he's not married. The stakes are suddenly higher and I wonder if there could be anything more between us.

"Throw out what you were going to do because there is something I need. I need you to come to hang out by the pumpkin launcher, drink hot cider, and keep on looking like a fall model." He reaches over and gives my forearm a squeeze. Electricity zaps me in the place our skin touches.

I laugh and shake my head. "You can't have all my time sir, I am at work."

"Fine, but I want you to find me when you take a break." He settles his arms across his broad chest and I can see the outline of his muscles through his thin shirt.

"I think I can do that." I can't help but smile up at him. I'm buzzing with butterflies.

"Okay." Taylor turns and heads back over to where his brothers impatiently wait. Then he pauses and looks back at me. "Molly, it's good to see you again. You've always been one of my favorites."

Chapter Two: Taylor

The day winds on and the guys and I have fun taking turns with the pumpkin launcher. As kids come through, we help them and their moms are generous with their donations. Since my divorce, I've had time to spend giving back to my community and it's become one of the things in life that makes me the happiest.

Running into Molly while doing it is another thing entirely. I've always liked Molly as a friend, but I was so wrapped up in my relationship with Christina, I never thought about her as anything more.

I've been on a few dates since my divorce, but nothing serious. Being with Molly today, I felt a definite spark. It hit me like a bolt of lightning. She's all grown up. Her straight body has morphed into one with thick curves. There's an inherent sexiness to her now that I never noticed before.

I make a point to watch her throughout the day. She keeps busy, that's for sure. Every interaction I see is a snapshot of the person she is and I can't get enough. She's helping an old woman to the car, pumpkin in tow. She's bouncing by on the hayride, chatting with a group of people, and offering to take a family photo for them. She's petting the goats. In short, Molly is adorable. Her smile is radiant, contagious even from here.

By the time she makes her way over to the pumpkin launcher, I'm practically crawling out of my skin ready to talk to her.

"There she is," I call out as she finally heads toward me. "Whoop!"

A red blush crawls across her cheeks and down the front of her shirt. I'd give anything to see where it ends.

"How's it going over here, gentlemen?"

"What's up Molly? How are you?" Patrick asks.

"I'm good, it's such a nice surprise to see you guys."

As she makes small talk with my brothers, I revel in the obvious comfort between them. I was there when her sister got sick. I brought her homework to her when she had to miss school. I remember the dark purple circles that took residence under her eyes when she would commute with her parents back and forth from the hospital.

Molly never complained. There wasn't anything she wouldn't do for Holly and their relationship reminded me of me with my own brothers, albeit a whole lot sweeter.

"You come over to launch a pumpkin or what?" Joshua asks.

"I don't know, I've got a few more tasks to check off before I'm done," she waves him away.

"Oh no, you're not getting off that easily. Come over here." I step toward Molly, take her clipboard, and place it on a bale of hay. "Pick a pumpkin to launch, sweetheart."

She looks up at me from underneath long, dark lashes, and her eyes sparkle in the golden sunlight. Then she takes a small pumpkin from the bin and holds it up. "Okay, let's do this."

I wrap my fingers around her wrist and pull her toward me. We walk to the furthest launcher. The enormous wooden poles are sunken into the ground and they cascade forty feet into the air. A black, rubber bungee is strung between them with a small leather pumpkin holder in the center.

"What in the world is all this? What do I do here?" Molly asks.

I can't help but let out a chuckle. "You've been in that city for far too long. Don't worry, I've got you."

I step behind her as she places her pumpkin on the leather holder. I run my hand down her arm and settle my hand on the back of hers as she grasps the bungee. Molly leans back against my chest and I feel her breathing sync with mine. It ignites me.

"Pull back," I whisper into her ear and she does. I don't want to let her go. "We'll let it go on three. One. Two—"

Before I can get to three, Molly releases the bungee and the thick cord rips her out of my arms propelling her forward. She lets out a loud yelp and lands on her back in the hay. In an instant, I'm rushing to her side.

"Are you okay?"

At first, she doesn't say anything and my heart rate ticks up. But then, I realize it's because she's laughing uncontrollably. The sound is loud and echoes in the open space. I can't help but join in as I lift her off the ground and put her back onto her feet.

We spend the rest of the evening launching pumpkins, chatting with my brothers, and helping customers as they come. Molly is the highlight of an already bright day.

When it's time to pack up, I insist on walking Molly to her car. When it's just the two of us standing in the golden orange sunset. I look into her eyes and I swear I see flashes of all that will be between us. It makes my heartbeat in my chest and I can't resist her for another minute.

Grabbing a hold of the front of her flannel with one hand, I tug her closer to me. I look into her eyes then plant my lips on hers and it sends a tingle whipping through my body.

I run my tongue over her lower lip and she parts her mouth, letting me inside. It's slow and passionate. When we part, we're both panting. Her breath rolls over my face, warm compared to the chilled evening air around us and I know nothing will ever be the same.

WHEN WE LEAVE BREW by Brewer for the day, I fight the urge to go on and on about Molly though I'm sure my brothers suspect that something's up. They're not wrong, something is up. Molly's all I can think about.

I find her on social media and after a few messages back and forth, we decide to just call. We spend the entire night on the phone. Molly and I catch up on every topic. My work as a firefighter. Her apartment in the city. My brothers. Her parents. But it doesn't stop there.

I learn that Molly hopes to move back to Misty Mountain to be near her aging parents. She hopes to get married and become a parent someday. She hopes to make an impact in her community. She hopes to leave this world better than she found it. She is incredible.

Molly is a supercharged version of her former self. I remember when she started dating Beans, he held her back, even talked down to her at times and it showed. She became a shell of her former self. Not anymore. The Molly I remember is back in my world, and now, she's drop-dead gorgeous to boot.

When we finally hang up, I know a few things for sure. I like Molly. I want her in my world for more than just these three days, and I'll do whatever I need to do to make it happen.

Chapter Three: Molly

The next morning, despite having stayed up on the phone all night with Taylor, I arrive early at the patch as planned. Being at my events from open to close is always a part of my plan but today, Taylor is all I can think about. I force myself to prioritize my commitments first.

I check in with Isabella, look over the activities schedule, and check-in with the Brewer staff. But once a staff member mentions that the firehouse guys have been scheduled to work the corn maze today, I'm a lost cause.

Immediately I start the trek through the pumpkin patch, past the petting zoo, and over to the cornfields. I can't get out there fast enough. I'm ready to see Taylor and buzzing with hopeful energy about what our future holds.

It seems Taylor's excited too because I'm not even halfway through the field yet when he starts jogging toward me.

"Good morning beautiful, I'm happy to see you." He plants a kiss on my cheek and it sends a red blush flushing across my face.

"Good morning." I chew on my lip. It's strange how someone I've known all my life can make me feel so nervous.

"Good morning princess," Joshua calls out in a high-pitched mocking tone and I can't help but laugh. The Henderson brothers are famous for poking fun at each other. Seeing their playful relationship makes me ache for my little sister.

"Ignore them. Besides, they won't be able to follow us in the maze, we'll be too fast." Taylor raises an eyebrow and a smile pulls at the corner of his mouth.

"What? Don't get me wrong, I love the idea of getting lost with you but It can take hours to get through the maze. I have a fundraiser to put on, this isn't a part of my plan for the day."

"I knew you wouldn't let me leave with you, but I have two cups of hot apple cider and a blanket. It's a fundraiser date. I think since we're selling tickets for this corn maze, the least we can do is work our way through it. Don't you agree?" A self-satisfied smile settles on his lips.

I consider his proposition. It seems he's got me on a technicality. It isn't really skirting my responsibilities to the fundraiser or breaking my commitments. I'll still be on property all day. "I guess I do." I let out a giggle.

"Come on," he wraps his hand around my wrist and pulls me toward the corn. Then he looks over his shoulder at his brothers. "We're headed somewhere far away from these bros." Joshua and Patrick laugh as we crunch our way through the soft hay between the rows of corn.

In an instant we're winding through the tall stalks, laughing and chasing each other like teenagers in love. I choose consistently wrong paths and Taylor laughs as we lose our way.

Then, he turns off the path and cuts a straight line out of the maze and into the wild rows of corn. The stalks shoot into the sky making us all but invisible to the rest of the world. But that's how it is when you're with Taylor, nothing else matters. He's all-encompassing and it's impossible to think about anything else.

Taylor pulls me into a soft kiss. His firm touch roams the back of my head. I look up at him from beneath my long, dark lashes and I can't believe we're here. I can't fathom that his lips are on mine.

"I never thought we'd get here—" I start but Taylor doesn't let me finish. Instead, he pulls my body back against his and seals the rest of my sentence with a long, passionate kiss.

Taylor sits onto the soft hay and pulls me down onto his lap. "Are you sure no one is going to wander through?" I can't help but feel a bit nervous, I've never done anything like this before.

His only response is a deep, throaty chuckle that comes out from between his teeth and a gentle tug on my arm. Another few minutes of being entangled with Taylor and it's hard to care about anything else.

Things start to blur after that. Taylor lays me on my back and climbs on top of me. He presses his weight down, using his arms to cage me in. His sizeable bulge catches between us as he moves on my body.

His mouth trails kisses up the sensitive nape of my neck. His pillowy lips tingle when they land on mine, eliciting rows of goosebumps in their wake. He parts my lips with his tongue. I feel his already firm length twitch with anticipation, pressing against the inside of his pants and begging to be freed. The heat of his skin against mine is electric.

He holds me there, loving on every inch of exposed skin he can find while I writhe against him with a desperate hunger for more. I run my hands up his chest, underneath his shirt, and across the taut muscles on his stomach. He makes quick work of unbuttoning my shirt and bra. My pants leave in a frenzy of pulling and tugging.

My heart rate picks up as my desire for him burns out of control. I pepper his neck with hungry kisses that only seem to heighten his excitement. Taylor squeezes my breasts then slips a needy nipple into his mouth, curling his tongue around the tip. It sends zaps of lightning through me as he suckles at my bud.

I reach out and grasp his member and it throbs in my hand. His tip is already glistening as I stroke him. His hands move slowly down my body, exploring every inch of skin before coming to rest between my legs and it makes pressure build low inside of me.

He cups my mound, fingers gently dancing across my slit. His touch is light, but it's enough to take my breath away. My body comes alive and I rock my hips against him. I ache with anticipation as Taylor pulls back onto his knees.

He rakes his tongue over me, licking and tasting. It sends a vibration of longing whipping through me and I have an overwhelming urge to have him inside of me. I don't have to wait long. When I whisper what I need from him, Taylor plunges his tongue deep inside my abyss and my body jumps in response.

He stays there for what seems like forever indulging me. Worshiping my curves. Tracing small circles across my swollen nub until I'm jumping with his every touch.

"You're ready for me aren't you?" His words are a raspy growl.

"Yes," I moan my reply and dig my fingers into the back of his scalp. I rock my hips up against his face one last time, then he sits back onto his knees.

Taylor puts a hand on my stomach and flips me over effortlessly onto all fours. I rear back toward him. He uses his knee to part my legs wider and I feel his firm length hot against my tight, puffy, lips. He slides his tip along my slit, teasing me until I beg for more.

Reaching back between my thighs, I tug on his balls and it ignites him. Taylor loses control, grabbing my hips and pushing into me with a single thrust. My walls stretch as he buries himself all the way inside of me. Once he's in, I can feel him pulsate.

Taylor slides in and out of me, slow at first then building into an intense rocking motion. Ripples of pleasure crawl across me. Soon I'm throwing my weight back into him and our bodies connect in perfect rhythm.

He keeps me there, heart-pounding and primal passion coursing through every inch of my body. I convulse with each fiery throb. Intense tremors build low inside of me as he pounds me into ecstasy.

Taylor hammers himself into me like he owns me and I'm all too happy to take it.

He smacks my ass and pulls my hair forcing me closer to the edge. I moan his name through clenched teeth until finally, I scream my release into the open field. My walls collapse along his length as I clench with each tremor of bliss that wracks my body.

Taylor lets go too and a guttural moan escapes from deep inside of him. I spread my legs wider, taking him in and milking him to the last drop as he rides a final wave of delirious pleasure.

When he collapses onto me, my body still tingles from his touch. I pant against him. I've never felt anything quite like this before. Being with him like this feels right. It's like we were always meant to be.

Chapter Four: Taylor

By early evening, I haven't had a chance to spend any more time with Molly but I'm still glowing from our romp in the corn. I feel protective of her, drawn to her, I've never been more sure about anything.

She's an amazing person and life with her in it looks somehow brighter than before. It's early, but something tells me this thing between us could be forever. I'm going to do everything in my power to make sure we get there.

When they release the volunteers for the day, I set out to find Molly. With her long golden locks blowing in the wind behind her, spotting her in the crowd doesn't take long. She's got her back to me. I hurry up the long dirt driveway to meet her. I won't take all of her time, but I at least want to kiss her goodbye.

As I get closer, I see she's engrossed in a conversation with a tall, skinny man who is more knees and elbows than anything else. He looks out of place in his white jeans, tan shirt, and manicured hair... but to each his own. With my brothers waiting for me to leave, I may have to settle for a wave from her.

"Molly," I call out but she doesn't seem to hear me.

My feet crunch on the path but I slow my pace as the man's face comes into view. I take a step back in surprise. It's Bradley Beans.

I haven't seen the dude in years, but you don't forget a face like that, smug, self-important, and shockingly arrogant. He lives in the city, I can't imagine what he's doing here. Seeing him that close to her doesn't sit right with me. I watch their interaction from a distance.

From the glimpses of her face I can see, she looks unsure, but not exactly unwilling to chat with him. He puts his hand on her shoulder. I don't like it and I can't tell whether she minds. It puts me on high alert. But neither of them looks like they're in a hurry so I stay back. I can't tear my eyes away.

The conversation between them seems to wind and shift. In response, my stomach swirls with the memory of the end of my marriage. The incident that brought the truth about my wife's affair to light started out much like this.

I blink and see an image of myself standing across the gym watching my then-wife interact with her personal trainer. Something prickled on the back of my neck, though I couldn't say what it was at the time. It didn't take long for the situation to become clear.

But Molly isn't my ex. In fact, Molly is quite the opposite, thoughtful, honest, and loyal to a fault. The truth settles like a knot over my chest. This conversation I'm watching is frankly, none of my business. I force myself to turn away, resigned to the idea of sending her a text message instead.

I take one last glance at the two of them. Molly turns her head toward me. Her face is pinched into tight lines and her hands fly up to cover her mouth. She looks upset, possibly even crying. Bradley takes a step closer to her and I've had enough.

My heart rate picks up. I'm not going to stand aside and let this happen. It might not be my place to step in, but I don't care. My feet are carrying me toward them faster than I can think.

"Hey, that's enough." My words punch out of me like a growl as soon as I'm in earshot and both of them turn with a start. I step beside Molly and put an arm around her neck, appraising her. There are definite tears in her eyes and it infuriates me. I turn to Bradley. "You can leave. We're done here."

"Who are you?" His face twists and turns then settles into an almost amused smirk.

"I'm the guy sending you on your way." My voice is loud and my brothers Patrick and Joshua must take notice because, in an instant, the two of them are marching toward us.

"What are you doing?" Molly looks up at me.

Before I respond, my brothers arrive on either side of Molly and me. The three of us Henderson brothers side by side form something of a wall. Combined, we must outweigh Bradley by nearly five hundred pounds of pure muscle, but he doesn't seem to notice.

Bradley lets out a wry chuckle. "What the hell is this? Wild. You mountain folks are really something."

"Everything okay over here?" Patrick's tone is cool and threatening.

Joshua lets out a loud chuckle of his own. "You're man enough to give her a hard time, but you don't want us to know about it? That's odd." He takes a step toward Bradley.

"What the hell are you doing?" Molly's voice rings out, puncturing the tension in the air. "Taylor, Bradley is making a donation. A sizable one at that. Why are you doing... whatever this is? This doesn't have anything to do with you."

My heart rate slows and I look at her. She stares up at me with an icy glaze and shrugs away from my touch.

"But you were crying." Doubt about what I saw swirls in my mind.

"I was taken aback by his generosity. It's amazing and this fundraiser is very close to home for me. So yes, I was crying." Molly's tone is cold.

My brother Patrick's eyes go wide. "Wow bro, looks like you're in trouble now. It seems like you've got it from here so we're gonna head out." I hear my brothers snicker to each other as they turn and head away from us as quickly as they arrived.

Bradley clears his throat. "Yeah, anyway, here's the check. I dedicated it to the memory of your sister Holly. I hope it goes a long way toward the new research wing of the hospital. And so sorry to cause such a... stir." He cuts his eyes at me and a smirk rests on his lips.

Bradley reaches out to hug Molly and it makes my blood boil. She pulls away quickly.

"Thank you, this means a lot," Molly says.

An awkward silence falls between the three of us and suddenly, all eyes are on me.

"What? He might be generous, but it doesn't make me like him any more than I did before." I furrow my eyebrows as I tell the simple truth.

Molly's face is unreadable.

Bradley crosses his arms over his chest and shakes his head. Then he looks past me to Molly. "Okay, I'm out of here. Good luck with the fundraiser and with... Whatever life choices you're making these days. Can't say I understand it much but... yeah."

He wanders away and when it's just she and I left, Molly gives me a stare so cold it could freeze water. I hold my hands up defensively, my heart rate ticks up, and adrenaline courses through me.

"I'm sorry." I blurt my words, already regretful of the scene I caused, though I stand by the purity of my intentions.

"You're supposed to be here helping to raise money. I know you hate your ex-wife, but I don't hate Bradley. He's a terrible boyfriend, sure. I don't even really want to be his friend honestly. But him deciding to donate money to this cause is bigger than my feelings for him. Can't you understand that?"

I swallow a lump in my throat. "I'm not gonna lie to you, I can understand that but I still don't like it. That guy treated you like—"

"It isn't any of your business." Molly's lips press into a tight, thin line and she forces a slow exhale through her nose. "I need to go. I have an event to finish."

"We need to talk about this, I'm not going to lose you before we even get started. So I was out of line but—" I start, but she turns away and shakes her head.

"I like you Taylor, and I know you well enough to understand where your weird energy is coming from, but I can't do this right now.

I know this fundraiser isn't personal for you, but it is for me. I already skirted some of my responsibilities by sneaking off with you earlier and I need to be present right now." Her words are clipped at the ends. "If you can't understand that, we have a much bigger problem."

"I do care about you, about this fundraiser, and about Holly's memory too. Don't forget, I was there and I hear you now. You have a late night here so we can talk tomorrow when I get here. Just please know I don't always handle things perfectly but it's coming from a good place."

"I know." She gives me a tight-lipped smile. "I'll see you tomorrow."

When she walks away, my stomach gurgles with anxiety. I need to find a way to show Molly exactly how much she means to me.

Chapter Five: Molly

I spend the night replaying the conversation with Taylor in my mind. By the time I wake up for the final day of the fundraiser, I've gotten some clarity on the situation.

Taylor is the exact same Taylor he's always been, intense, loyal, and protective. Those aren't bad qualities. I think about what it must have been like for him to see me standing there with Bradley. I can't blame Taylor for his reaction, and I can't wait to see him and clear the air between us.

I head out to the pumpkin patch at Brew by Brewer bright and early. I check in with Isabella Brewer and double-check the agenda for the day. It seems everything is in place, yet I still feel on edge and Taylor isn't anywhere to be seen.

As the day winds on, the sun sets over the pumpkin patch just as brilliantly vibrant as it's ever been. The colors don't hold my attention the way they have in the last two days. Or at least, they don't fill me with the same sense of peace they normally do.

Instead, I'm fixated on the fact that all three Henderson brothers are noticeably absent from the firefighter volunteer crew. I know the way Taylor and I left things was uncomfortable but I never took him for the kind of person who would just disappear. He's breaking a commitment he made to help raise funds for the hospital. It's not like him and it isn't okay with me.

By the time Isabella takes the stage to share the final figures for our fundraising efforts, my stomach is in knots. I pull my phone out of my back pocket and punch out a text message to Taylor.

Me: *Is everything okay? I wanted to talk today.*

Taylor: *We will. Need time.*

I don't know what his text means to be honest. Time? What does that mean? A day? A week? A year? Is this his nice-guy way of letting me down easy so he can never talk to me again? I wonder what his plan is because, for the first time in a long time, I don't have a plan of my own.

Me: *Okay*

I read the message over and over again. His four words send me into a tailspin. I don't understand what he's doing. Maybe Taylor isn't the same person I knew after all. First, he's swooping in to save me from a situation that is fully under control. Then he's telling me we need to talk through our issues on the spot. Now he needs more time and has all but vanished.

Isabella's voice in the microphone brings me back to the present. "I'd like to thank everyone for coming tonight. The donations we received exceeded our expectations. We're incredibly grateful to be a part of this event. I'm pleased to announce on behalf of my family that Brew by Brewer will match the sum total of the donation with a donation of our own."

Applause rings out across the crowd and I can't help but join in. Despite how things are between Taylor and me. The event was a success and that is something to be proud of.

Isabella continues, "We also have another surprise announcement."

I raise my eyes to the stage, my interest piqued. Whatever she's about to say is news to me too.

She continues, "Thanks to a generous donation of time and a whole lot of sweat equity, the garden cottage outside of the hospital is undergoing a month-long process of renovation. The cottages will be transformed into guest quarters to house the families of the patients in the children's wing of Francis hospital."

My eyes go glassy. These cottages will change the lives of so many families. They'll be a place of rest and rejuvenation, a symbol of hope in the darkest of times. I swallow the lump in my throat as she continues.

"The firehouse has taken on this project out of an abundance of generosity. Work started yesterday and they will have crews working around the clock until the project is complete. We have a few photos of the progress. We'll project them on the side of the barn in just a minute here..."

Taylor needs time because he's out at the hospital working on the cottages. My heart melts.

Isabella fumbles with her phone and a man dashes over to the projector. All the while, my heart is pounding in my chest. Taylor is exactly who he has always been. I know he's behind this and I can't believe I doubted him even for a minute.

Then, photo after photo flashes onto the screen. The cottages. Tractors. Firefighters grinning holding bags of cement. Patrick and Joshua smiling at the camera carrying bricks into the dead of night. Taylor installing a sign at the garden's entrance that reads, *The Holly Houses.*

Tears stream down my cheeks. It's the most thoughtful thing anyone has ever done for me and it means so much. As Isabella continues to show pictures of the project all I can think about is talking to Taylor. I pull my phone out of my pocket to send him a text but before I can, I feel a hand on my shoulder.

I turn to look up at Taylor, butterflies flapping wildly in my stomach. "Thank you, I can't believe you made this happen. It's so sweet."

He wraps his arms around me and plants a soft kiss on my forehead. I relax into the safety and warmth of his embrace.

"I want you to know that I take this seriously. I might not have the means to cut a six-figure check to the foundation, but I know how to make an impact. I had them plant giant sunflowers outside of the bedroom windows because I remember that they were Holly's favorite. There will be butterflies and hummingbirds, all the things I thought you would have liked back when you were in that situation."

"That cottage would have changed my life as a child. Holly would have loved it." My words catch in my throat as I think about my little sister.

"I'm sorry I overreacted yesterday. It's just that I'm falling for you hard and fast. I want to give this a chance with you and even if it isn't me, you deserve a lot better than Bradley. Dude wore white pants to a pumpkin patch."

I can't help but giggle. "Agree. But I don't think I'll have to worry about it. I think it will be you and I until the end."

We seal our words with a sweet kiss. The autumn wind sends brown leaves swirling around us. The breeze washes away the past and sends Taylor and me arm and arm into our future.

Epilogue: Molly, One Year Later

"What about this one?" Taylor holds up a white pumpkin. "I like it, but it isn't the one I'm looking for. I have something very specific in mind."

Taylor, patient as ever, isn't deterred. He holds up pumpkin after pumpkin. He nods his head with hopeful anticipation. With each one, I shake my head regretfully. I force myself to bite back my smile as he takes my hand in his. My stomach bubbles with excitement.

Taylor and I step through the muddy pumpkin patch in our rubber boots. As we hike, my eyes roam the rolling hills of vined pumpkins. The golden sun setting over the hill is a breathtaking sight, but I'm only searching for one thing, a scarecrow. I put in a call to Isabella Brewer and she's got it all set up for me, now all I have to do is get Taylor and I to the top of the hill so we can find it.

The last year by Taylor's side has been filled with a million memories just like this. Me dreaming, imagining, and planning. Taylor tirelessly bringing everything to life. He proposed to me just two weeks after we reconnected that day at the charity event. I said yes immediately, without a plan. I just knew it was right.

We held a simple wedding ceremony the following week. I remember it like it was yesterday. My dad walked me down the aisle on a beautiful fall day out in the patch at Brew by Brewer. White pumpkins lined on either side of me formed an aisle. Taylor and I were surrounded only by our closest family and friends.

It was magic. The memories of that day wrap around me like a cozy knit blanket on an early fall night. Taylor is everything I was too afraid to hope for, but his unscheduled arrival in my life was right on time.

Now I'm brimming with joy because I get to return the favor. Today I'll make one of Taylor's dreams come true. As we come up over the top of the hill, my eyes settle on the brown hat belonging to a man made out of straw. A broad smile stretches across my face.

"That's it. Right over there below the scarecrow, that's the pumpkin I want." I have to stop myself from breaking into a full sprint. I gesture across the field and Taylor turns to follow my gaze.

"Okay, a perfect pumpkin for my pumpkin. Let's go get you the one you want." Taylor kisses my forehead and warmth blooms low in my stomach.

I interlace my fingers with his and pull him toward the scarecrow. When we finally reach our destination, my eyes brim with tears. I make a mental note to thank Isabella. It's absolutely perfect. Three white pumpkins are stacked on top of each other to form a tower. I read the words written on each pumpkin from bottom to top.

Dad. Mom. Baby Henderson.

When I look at Taylor, he's already blinking back tears. "Are you?"

I nod. "I am." I put a hand low on my belly.

"I'm so happy." His words are nothing more than a breathy whisper. His hand settles on top of mine. "I'm going to be a dad."

"I think it's a girl... it's just a hunch."

Taylor's tears give way to a smile that curls the corners of his mouth. In an instant, my feet are dangling in midair as Taylor lifts me off the ground in a fierce hug.

This baby will come into the world fiercely loved. In a flash, I see glimpses of our future as a family of three, pumpkin patches, hayrides, spooky Halloween nights, and merry Christmas mornings.

I want all of it. The good, the bad, the organized, the unplanned. But I can't imagine doing any of it without Taylor by my side. Together he and I will confidently take a perfectly imperfect step into forever.

Crisp Kiss, Chapter One: Patrick

"You can head over to the petting zoo, Cassie will meet you there," Isabella says. "She's one of our longtime volunteers."

All of the employees at the Brew by Brewer pumpkin patch have been exceptionally friendly. But from what I can tell, Isabella is responsible for everything and I'm here to help, so I jump at her request.

"Yes ma'am. I'll see you boys later," I give my brothers a nod.

As I make my way from the barn across the pumpkin patch, the crisp fall air washes over me. Three days of volunteering here for charity ain't so bad. Besides, it's either this or hanging out at the station. So I'm happy to be here with the other firefighters donating my time to an event that benefits our local hospital.

I step through the makeshift corral and into what I assume is the petting zoo. It isn't much. Just some chickens in a large pen, one alpaca, two pigs, and a few goats. When I approach the goat pen, two of them rush up to greet me. They're no doubt disappointed that I don't have food for them, but I crouch down and reach through the horse fencing to pet them anyway.

"Excuse me, we aren't open yet." A woman's syrupy sweet voice comes from over my shoulder.

I turn and see a pair of thick thighs tucked into jeans so tight they could be painted on. My eyes involuntarily run up her body as I get to my feet. She's curvy in all the right places. When my eyes land on her face, there's no missing the fact that she's beautiful. Her skin is copper kissed from the sun. Her dark hair is pulled back into a low ponytail.

My first thought is, *her body and her face make a stunning combination.* This is immediately followed by my next thought, *please don't let this be Cassie because she looks young, real young.*

The woman trains her huge, almond-shaped, brown eyes on me. From the way they light up as she looks me up and down, I already know I'm in trouble. I force my eyes to stay locked onto her face.

"I'm Patrick Henderson with the Misty Mountain fire department. I'm here to help."

"Cassie Bryan," is all she says.

Dammit. So much for it not being her.

I extend my hand. When she takes it, a tingle runs up and down my spine. "Why haven't I met you before? Misty Mountain isn't exactly a huge place."

"I just moved here. I'm living with my Gram."

With her Gram? Oh shit, she's not even legal. I've got to get another assignment.

"For high school?" The words catch in my throat. At thirty-six, I'm a senior citizen by comparison.

Cassie lets out a long, hearty laugh. "No. No worries there, I'm legal you can relax. I'm twenty-four. I moved here because I love small-town life. I've always wanted to move here to be close to my grandparents. Come on, let me show you around."

My mouth falls open. Am I that transparent? I'm really off my game.

I follow Cassie into the back of the barn. She goes through a list of items that I'm unfamiliar with, explaining in detail what each one does. *This is for the goats. This is what we give the pigs. Here's where we put the hay bales.* But all I can focus on is the way her full, pouty, lips turn up at the corners with each word she says.

An hour later and I still haven't exactly found my footing with her, but that doesn't stop Cassie from putting me to work. I'm cleaning out cages and feeding the alpaca while she chit-chats with me and the pigs. There's extraordinary confidence about her that I can't help but be drawn to.

Ding.

When the timer sounds from the phone in her pocket, Cassie holds it up toward me. "It's time! Come look at this group... just babies."

She hurries out of the barn's back door and onto the screened porch. I follow closely behind her marveling at the way her ass bounces with each step she takes. In the center of the patio is a basket with three tiny kittens inside.

"Someone found them abandoned in the patch so I've been taking turns with a few of the other volunteers bottle feeding them. Do you want to help?" Cassie scoops up an orange cat so tiny its eyes are hardly open and cradles it against her chest. She's a natural, the kitten calms against Cassie immediately.

Lucky cat.

"Wow, they're so small. Pretty adorable too. Poor things left to fend for themselves like that. It's lucky they have you." I sit down on the floor beside Cassie and trace my finger down the soft fur of a white kitten still tucked into the basket. When she cries, her meow is nothing more than a soft whimper.

"Come here, sweetheart." I melt as I pick up the kitten in my palm. "You're so precious."

"Aww," Cassie says, and I can't help but laugh at myself.

I deepen my voice dramatically. "I mean, come on now kitten, I'll save you. Cass, next time you've got to give me a man's job like moving something or building something. Don't you know what to do with a real man?" I flex my bicep and smirk at her expecting to draw a blush to her cheeks.

Instead, she arches an eyebrow at me and her mouth pulls up on one side. "Ha, well, I've never had one before, but I like the sound of it." She bites her lower lip and it drives me wild.

Just like that, she's put me on my heels again. I'm so intrigued by this stunning woman. Cassie and I sit with the kittens and rotate them through a cycle of bottle feeding. I don't miss the fact that she leans into me a little too long and she doesn't pull away when I rest my thigh next to hers.

There's a live electrical current running between us. I learn that Cassie is an only child who grew up in the city with her corporate America parents. Her Gram is her favorite person and Cassie loves to bake.

She's different from most of the women I've dated and certainly the opposite of my ex-wife. Cassie is direct. She laughs at my cheesy jokes and she has her finger on the pulse of who she is and who she wants to be.

Every sentence out of her mouth draws me in more than the last. When the feeding is done, neither of us is in a rush to get up. Instead, Cassie and I sit side by side falling in love with the tiny kittens, and dare I say, with each other.

"Can I ask you something, if you aren't here for school, then what are you doing here?" I can't help but want more detail. I want to know everything about her.

"Finding a husband."

I wait for the punchline, but Cassie's face is dead serious. I arch my eyebrows up in surprise and a chuckle escapes my lips. "What the hell, Cass? I don't think you're supposed to say that out loud."

"Why? People talk about the things they want all the time. They want a job or a certain car. Well, I just want the simple, boring life I never got to have growing up. A husband that works. A simple house. Kids I get to stay home and raise. I think a better question might be, why does it make you uncomfortable? Are you worried you might be him?" She looks at me, a teasing, flirty, smile resting on her lips.

"What if I'm worried I might *not* be him?" Now it's her turn to look taken aback. "But seriously, you wouldn't want me in the long term. Us Henderson brothers don't have a great track record for divorce. I tried being a husband once and it didn't last long."

"Because?" Cassie nods expectantly.

"A lot of reasons I guess, but when you have two people who both care about making a living, there isn't anyone available to make a life. She loved her job and I was fine with that until it became clear she loved it more than she loved me." My divorce was so long ago at this point, it feels like I'm talking about someone else's life.

Beep. Beep.

Cassie's two-way radio sounds before she can respond and Isabella's voice crackles on the speaker. "Cassie?"

She pulls the radio to her mouth. "Yes."

"Please send the firefighter volunteers over to the pumpkin launcher."

On a whim, I reach over Cassie and pull the radio from her hand. She looks at me, her mouth falling open.

I push the talk button. "Nah. I don't like the idea. Over."

"What?" Isabella's voice chirps back at me.

Cassie bats me away with a laugh and leans over me to reach for the radio while I hold it at arm's length. Finally, I roll my eyes and hold the talk button down for her.

"No problem, he'll be right over," Cassie calls into the speaker.

With her body sprawled across my lap like this, my heart pounds out of control. Without giving it another thought, I lean down and plant my lips on hers. It's sweet and chaste but it sucks up all the air on the screened porch anyway.

I take her face in my hands, and when I finally open my eyes, Cassie is all I see.

BY LATE AFTERNOON, we are slammed with customers. I spend the rest of my day at the pumpkin patch hustling through a million tasks and stealing glances at Cassie. I offer to make deliveries across the property just to walk by her station. I never stop thinking about the way her body felt pressed up against mine.

When it's time to go home, I feel a pang of disappointment when I find out Cassie's already gone home for the day. But on the upside, volunteering at the fundraiser for another two days just got a whole lot more interesting.

Chapter Two: Cassie

I sleep in on day two of the fundraiser for Francis Hospital and head to the pumpkin patch in the afternoon for my scheduled shift. I suppose I was exhausted from the thoughts of Patrick that danced in my head all night. If I ever had even one moment of doubt about my decision to move to Misty Mountain, spending my days volunteering has put them at rest.

There's something thrilling about watching families come running through, looking for the perfect pumpkin. I just love it. All the happy smiles on the faces of the kids bring me so much joy. I love to see the adults come through too, especially the ones that grew up in a city all their life like I did. They come here and get wrapped up in the marvel of nature.

I have a soft spot for autumn, it's my favorite time of the year. The leaves are on the ground. The smell of it. I could breathe in autumn air all year round and be happy. The addition of the sexy firefighters to the equation is a definite bonus. I didn't expect Patrick, but it's like something in me recognized him right away.

I know he's meant to be a part of my life, in the same way, I knew moving to Misty Mountain was it for me. It's like I've been waiting for him and now that he's arrived in my world, I can't think about anything else.

When I check in with Isabella, she hands me my radio. Then she asks me to head out to the pumpkin patch which works out perfectly because Gram is meeting me here in just a bit. She's dead set on taking a hayride this afternoon no matter how bumpy it is. When the woman decides she's going to do something, there isn't any changing her mind.

I walk through the pumpkin patch, ensuring all the exit signs are pointing in the right direction and making sure there isn't any garbage on the ground. It's serene. I could walk out here all day. But when I see the entrance to the hayride, I make my way over to wait for Gram.

The ride is really just a large green wagon hooked up to the back of a tractor. The wagon is covered and piled full of hay bales that are arranged to be a sort of sitting area. But my stomach twists a bit when I see the high steps required to climb into the covered wagon. I know Gram won't admit that they may be a challenge for her and I don't want her to hurt herself.

"What's going on Cinderella? You waiting for one of these pumpkins to turn into a prince?" Patrick's voice behind me brings an immediate grin to my face and sends butterflies flapping in my stomach.

"I was hoping I'd see you! I'm not the type to wait for a prince. I'm more of the go out and find him type." I look up at Patrick and he wraps me into a warm hug. "How are you?"

"Better now that I found you. What are you up to over here?" Patrick drapes an arm over my shoulder and it just feels right.

"You see that woman waving wildly? That's Gram." I point at Gram making her way up from the parking lot and Patrick follows my line of sight. "She's come all the way down here just for a hayride. So I guess I'm helping her into that wagon." Patrick turns and gives Gram a hearty wave.

"If you wave, you've got to stick around and meet her," I giggle.

"Are you kidding me? I can't wait to meet that legend. I'm personally escorting the two of you onto this hayride."

Ten minutes later and I've made the official introduction. Patrick is dazzling with his brilliant smile and disarming humor. I can tell Gram is charmed to her core and I couldn't be more pleased with the way this is going.

When it's our turn, the tractor is still running and the man on it has a pair of earmuffs on. He waves us aboard and I eye the steps. Patrick puts a hand on my waist to move me aside. Then he stands behind Gram and all but lifts her right onto the wagon.

She lets out a giggle of surprise but she doesn't seem to mind and I swell with relief. Then Patrick helps me on board in the same way and I can't help but laugh. He climbs onto the wagon behind me and the three of us get settled at the very back.

When we sit, the hay is scratchier than I thought, poking at me even through the backs of my jeans. I sit between Gram and Patrick and I can't help but think that this could be the first of many times I could find myself in this delightful situation. Surrounded by people who make me smile.

Gram's attention is immediately trained out into the fields, but I am barely sitting before the tractor jerks into motion bumping me into Patrick's solid body. The sounds of the pumpkin patch are almost swallowed up by the grumbling groan of the tractor.

We wind through the front half of the farm, and then out onto the main road on a dirt trail. Either side is lined with autumn-colored trees, and with the sun setting around us, it makes for a breathtaking ride.

Even more so when Patrick rests his hand on top of my thigh, fingers running lightly over the inseam of my jeans. My heart skips a beat. I risk a glance at Gram, but she is totally unaware of anything other than the pumpkin patch.

Patrick has to lean right up into my personal space to be heard over the sound of the tractor engine. His lips brush over my ear as he tells me how beautiful I am in the golden sunlight. When he turns his head to the side, I give him a peck on the cheek.

As we bounce around the patch, I check in with Gram who appears to be having the time of her life. We wind around the Brewer property, past the brewery, past the cat cafe, and it all feels so magical.

By the time the barn comes back into sight, I've got one hand on the inside of Patrick's thigh, steadily creeping along the inseam up toward the noticeable bulge in his jeans. Teasing. Tempting. But never touching, not with Gram right beside me at least.

The hayride stops where it started and I don't want it to end. Patrick helps us out of the wagon effortlessly.

"Well, you two are sweet to take an old lady with you on your date." Gram winks and it makes me flush red with embarrassment.

"If it's a date, I should get you something to eat. I think they have fried... everything over there. What do you say?" Patrick asks, not missing a beat.

"No honey, you two can walk me to my car. This is about enough excitement for me for one day," Gram says.

Patrick offers her his elbow and it makes my heart melt when she slips her frail arm through it. I walk a few paces behind them and watch as Gram falls in love with my future husband.

Chapter Three: Cassie

After we see Gram off, Patrick and I can't keep our hands off each other. We manage to make it past the makeshift fence of hay bales set up around the patch and into the back forty. There are still pumpkins, but we're so far out, the area has been largely untouched by patrons of the patch.

By the time the barn fades into the distance, I just can't stand it anymore. I turn to Patrick, shoving my hands up under the front of his shirt and leaning in for a kiss. After that, it's a whole lot less talking and a whole lot more hands roaming. But what starts out as innocent and chaste doesn't last long.

"Slow down Cass, I shouldn't be doing this."

His words are hard to believe when his bulge is hitting me in the stomach. "I don't think you mean that do you?" I run my hand down his stomach and down the front of his pants.

"Nope. I sure don't," his words are a breathy moan.

In an instant, I'm pushing him backward. Patrick goes down willingly, settling on his back in the middle of the pumpkin patch and I'm on my knees, reaching for his zipper. When I break it free from his zipper, I grasp his firm length and Patrick drops his head back, letting it hang between his shoulders and groans.

I run my tongue over the length of his shaft, then curl my lips just barely around the head of it. I like the way his cock hits the back of my throat when I take him into my mouth. I like the way he tries to control himself by curling his hands up in the thick layer of straw that tops the soil. I like the way he looks into my eyes while I lick him.

I keep a tight grip on his hips, holding him down so he knows that I'm in charge right now. With each bob, I take a little more of him into my mouth, curling my tongue so it presses up against the underside of his tip.

I pull back so I can mouth at his balls, then slide him all the way into my mouth. I move slowly, teasing, watching him squirm. Patrick's hips jerk. His muscles bunch up and tense as I take even more of him into my mouth.

"You're going to kill me if you keep this up," he groans a laugh, one arm thrown over his face.

I bob back down on his cock and hollow out my cheeks. From the way he tries to roll his hips in response, I can tell he likes it and it spurs me on. His hands are in my hair. His words come out as a garbled moan of my name. A desire for him builds low in my stomach.

"I'm not ready yet," he growls.

Patrick pulls me up by my hair and when our lips meet, he parts my mouth with hungry desperation. Our tongues dance as our kiss deepens and passion erupts between us. Without taking his mouth off me, he unbuttons my jeans and tugs them off my hips.

He runs a hand between my legs and along my glistening slit, parting my folds. Patrick moves deliberately, taking his time with me, and my body tremors in response. This man knows exactly what he's doing.

He traces circles on my swollen nub. A smoldering intensity runs through my body and I roll my hips hard against his touch. My walls pulsate, desperate to be filled by him and I can hardly catch my breath.

From there, it's a blur. With a rush of movement, I'm on top of him. I straddle his large body and my chest presses into his. I stare down at him, my face framed by my wild hair, our hearts beating in unison.

Patrick slides his large hands around my thighs, steadying me. I hover over him, his tip knocking against my opening. Then let out a sharp exhale as he plunges all the way inside of me. I stay still for a moment as my walls stretch to accommodate his sizable girth.

Then I rock onto him, slow and sensual. His eyes roll back into his head. I pick up the pace, my rocking grows into a hard and fast bounce. My desire for Patrick burns frantically, driving us together.

Our bodies become one, a current of wild electricity crackling between us. Pressure builds in me and every muscle I have tightens. His hands are on my hips, on my mounds, and twisting my nipples.

My hands are under his shirt, tracing the outline of his taut muscles. We settle into an intense rhythm as he pulsates inside of me. Patrick works me into a fervor, rhythmic tremors coming on faster and faster. My breathing grows erratic as he pushes me toward the edge.

Intense pleasure takes me over. I arch my spine, driving my hips into him as I give in. My walls collapse along his length with trembling waves of pleasure and I bear down as my body convulses. I moan my release into the open sky.

Patrick lets out a loud moan of his own then grunts. He pounds his throbbing member into me and shoots hot streams as he lets go. I tighten my walls around him and milk him to the last drop.

Chapter Four: Patrick

I could lay here like this, with Cassie's beautiful, half-naked body on me forever. But the sound of footsteps crunching toward us bursts us out of our blissful bubble.

"Oh damn!" Cassie looks up at me, her hair disheveled, and a giddy grin on her lips.

I'm still trying to catch my breath when Cassie squirms back into her jeans and buttons her flannel shirt. I pull on the top of my pants, tugging them up quickly enough that I don't even get the straw out of them first.

"This isn't how I wanted to end my time with you," I chuckle.

"Well these people only paid six dollars a ticket, I don't want them to see more than they bargained for," she giggles. "I know it's for charity, but still."

I can't help but laugh as we make our way out of the pumpkin patch. I sling an arm over Cassie's shoulder and kiss the top of her head. Having her tucked into my side feels right. Cassie is fun and sweet, not to mention sexy as hell. I'm overwhelmed with an urge to take care of her and keep her safe.

"So how would you have liked to end our time together?" She looks up at me with those wide, sparkling eyes that I can't resist.

"First of all, I wouldn't want it to end at all. But if it had to, I'd say that it should probably be with a pumpkin scone." I brush a strand of hair away from her face.

"Wait, what? Guys don't think about pumpkin scones, especially firefighters. You're teasing me," she giggles.

"Not at all. My mom is famous for her seasonal baked goods. Especially fall and her scones in particular. I once asked my mom if she regretted not having a daughter, I mean three boys couldn't have been easy. She told me her only disappointment was not having anyone to bake with. So from that moment on, I decided I would be that person for her. Now, when fall rolls around, you name a baked good, I can make it happen. She passed along her pumpkin scone recipe, but I have to guard the secret. So, I'd like to end our time together by making you breakfast. It's a little late for today, I guess, but what about tomorrow?"

"That's the sweetest thing I've ever heard. I'd love to have breakfast with you tomorrow." Cassie's mouth curls into a smile and she clasps her hands in front of her chest. "Wait, tomorrow's Sunday isn't it? I have breakfast with Gram every Sunday morning. We'll have to pick another day. Besides, I'm working here at the fundraiser again tomorrow."

I'm not letting her off the hook that easily. "So I'll meet you here. Bring Gram. The three of us will have breakfast. I'll meet you two with a batch of pumpkin scones you'll never forget. What do you say?" Problem solved. Besides, I want to be around for a long time and that means getting to know Cassie's family.

I don't have to wait for her reply, the smile on Cassie's face as she looks up at me says it all.

"That settles it. I'll meet you bright and early at the picnic tables under the pergola, around eight?"

"It's a date," Cassie says.

MY DAY OF VOLUNTEERING flies by and they sure do keep us busy. We are everywhere. Helping load pumpkins into cars. Helping launch pumpkins into the field. Helping to feed the chickens. But with as much running around as we're doing, you can hardly call this work.

It's a lot of fun to be outside on another beautiful fall day. My brothers and I are no strangers to hard work. We banter back and forth while pitching in anywhere we can. It's for a good cause, but I don't feel like this is much of a contribution.

By late afternoon, I'm still riding a high from my romp with Cassie in the patch. I'm using a wheelbarrow to move pumpkins for a family of five when my older brother Taylor bounds toward me. His face is pinched into lines and his eyebrows furrow in the center. I keep my eyes trained on him. I can tell he wants something and I know from experience that once he gets his mindset on an idea, there isn't any saying no to him.

I get the family situated and as soon as they're out of sight, I turn to Taylor. "What do you need?"

"Get Joshua over here, I have an idea but I need all three of us and possibly some guys from the station," Taylor says.

"Oh boy, this should be good," I chuckle.

An hour later, Taylor's hands fly as he talks, hatching a plan to enhance our contribution to the hospital's project. He wants to round up a crew and take an overnight trip to Francis Hospital. Apparently, they've got some cottages in their gardens that he thinks would work well as guest cottages for the family members of chronically ill patients. The man's insane, but there isn't any way I would say no.

We make some calls and mobilize quickly. The next thing I know, I'm in a truck with my brothers and we're making the long drive out to the hospital. We stay up all night making dreams come to life and all I can think is that *this* is what a true donation of time looks like.

Adrenaline carries us straight through the night. Despite the fact that we're lifting, planting, and demolishing, I don't even feel tired, at least not until we're back in the truck. The sun is already peeking out over the clouds as we rumble down the road toward Misty Mountain.

"Are you good to drive?" Taylor asks Joshua.

"Yeah, I'm not as old as you two." Joshua lets out a wry chuckle. "I'm okay. Honestly, I haven't been this tired in a good while."

"I can take a turn if you need," I tell him.

When we pass the first exit for Misty Mountain, all three of our phones chime simultaneously. The guys and I look at each other.

"It's either Mom or the station," I say.

"Oh no, I don't know which to hope for," Joshua laughs as he pulls onto the off-ramp.

I dig my phone out of my pocket. "It's the station. It's not good, looks like we're at level zero. We've got to get another engine up and they need bodies. Any volunteers?" I ask.

"I was going to head back out to the hospital project but I can make it work," Taylor says, but I can tell his heart isn't in it. The project out at the hospital is his idea and I know he wants to see it through.

"I've got a shift at ten already, but I can head in early," Joshua offers. As soon as the words leave his mouth I know that won't work either. Turning a fourteen-hour shift into a twenty-hour shift is unbearable, especially if we're busy.

"No, neither one of you is going in. I've got it. I'll run a couple of calls until we get caught up and then I'll sleep." I end the conversation and send a text letting the chief know that I'll be in before my brothers can protest.

The truth is, I'm still floating on air from my time with Cassie. As long as I have enough time to bake a batch of scones before eight, I feel like I could never sleep again.

Chapter Five: Cassie

The next morning, a solid thirty minutes pass as Gram and I sit at the tables under the pergola waiting for Patrick. With each passing moment, my chest tightens a little more.

"Is he okay?" Gram asks a half-smile resting on her lips.

"I'm sure. I'll just shoot him a quick text." My casual tone betrays the pounding in my chest as I dig my phone out of my bag.

8:32 Me: *Hey, are you on your way?*

8:40 Me: *You didn't forget about Gram and me did you?*

But no response comes.

It feels unreal to me that Patrick, who seemed so different from anyone I've ever met, could be just another man who ends up letting me down.

For a moment, I let my body sag against the pole that holds up the pergola. The metal is cool against my hot skin burning with embarrassment. I fight the urge to groan audibly. This situation would have been devastating on its own.

Being stood up the day after you impulsively sleep with someone in a pumpkin patch isn't anyone's idea of a good time. But why did he have to stand me up in front of Gram? I know she already worries about me, and this isn't going to do anything to build her confidence in my ability to choose quality men.

I think through my options in an effort to find what's going to be less mortifying. I could make up an excuse for him, but I'm not sure he deserves that. I could act like it hasn't impacted me, though I'm not sure she'd believe it anyway. In the end, I settle on buying Gram a pumpkin muffin and silently cursing my decision to fall headfirst for a man who seemed too good to be true.

"You haven't heard from him at all this morning, have you?" Gram asks, a sympathetic smile resting on her lips.

"No. You must think I'm a terrible picker, but honestly, this is the first time I've fallen so hard so fast. I really thought Patrick was different." It's no use trying to keep up appearances with the woman who knows me best in the world. I let my shoulders slump forward as the truth pours out of me.

"I don't think that at all. In fact, I think you are right. I think he's different. Charming. Handsome to be sure. But he's still a man. Sometimes you have to give a little grace. He'll contact you, and when he does, hear him out. It might still end with the two of you parting ways, but he might have a reason too. We have no way of knowing right now, do we? Then we can decide whether or not you're a bad picker. " Gram chuckles as she breaks the corner off her muffin and pops it into her mouth.

"How old were you before you got wise?" I tease her with a giggle.

GRAM HEADS HOME AND I start my shift at the pumpkin patch in the petting zoo. We are busier than yesterday. As the day winds on, I try to focus on the importance of the fundraiser. Donating to the hospital is certainly a worthy cause and a good reminder of all the things I have to be grateful for. With that in mind, I push myself. I help kids through the petting zoo. Take care of the animals, and run errands for Isabella all across the vast Brewer property.

As the morning winds on, I'm keeping busy, but none of it takes my mind off Patrick. It's nearly eleven o'clock and still, I've heard nothing from him. I guess he really will be just another name on the list of disappointments.

Beep. Beep.

I'm filling the goat's pen with fresh hay when my two-way radio makes a sound.

"Cass?" Isabella's voice crackles through the speaker.

"Yes."

"Can you meet me under the pergola as soon as possible please?"

Well, at least someone wants to meet me under the pergola. My stomach sinks. The irony is just too much. "No prob, I'm heading right over."

Before I go, I can't help but check my phone again, just in case I missed a message from Patrick, but alas, nothing. I close the goat's pen and make my way across the patch. I can't believe he's actually going to ghost me.

I make my way around to the pergola, but as I close in on the picnic tables, Isabella isn't anywhere to be seen. Instead, there's an enormous spread of baked goods on tiered trays, muffins, pastries, and suspiciously... scones.

I pick up a still-warm scone and when I bite into it, the taste of pumpkin spice melts in my mouth. It's delicious. The kind of recipe that gets handed down from mother to child. My heartbeat picks up.

I know I shouldn't let myself get too excited, because what if it's not him? What if this spread is a part of the fundraiser, just a happy coincidence? My hands tremble with nerves as I pick up my two-way radio and push the talk button. "Isabella?"

"No, sorry. It's just me." Patrick's voice comes from behind me and I jump with a start. When I turn, he's standing just a few feet from me, a sheepish smile on his face.

"What are you doing?" I ask, my mouth falling open. "I was waiting for you and checking my phone like an idiot."

"This is my apology. I'm so sorry I missed this morning, it isn't like me. I can explain exactly what happened if you'll let me. I can't imagine what you must have thought sitting out here waiting for me, I hate that I did that to you. I figured a pumpkin scone was my best shot at getting you to hear me out." His words come out fast and in a jumble. He seems so much different from the cool collected man I've gotten to know over the last couple of days.

"Well, that's a good start." My mouth pulls into a cautious, tight-lipped smile.

The short story is, he set an alarm but didn't wake up until two hours ago. But as we sit together at a picnic table surrounded by the pumpkin treats Patrick baked in the last hour, he tells me the long version.

Patrick explains that the fire department has taken on a community service project out at the hospital as a part of this event. He drove to Francis Hospital in the dead of night and worked with his brothers until the sun came up only to be called into work at the fire station upon his return.

He scrolls through the pictures on his phone that validate everything he's telling me. But he doesn't need to. There isn't any doubt in my mind that Patrick's telling the truth. As he talks, he's genuine, sincere, and apologetic. More than that, he's supposed to be mine. I just know it.

"As soon as I opened my eyes, I saw the sun burning through my window and I knew I messed this up. I'm sorry. I can't imagine what you must have felt." He takes my hand and interlaces our fingers.

Heat bubbles up under my palm. "I was disappointed, but I do understand. I wish you would have texted me."

"I do too and I will if anything like this ever happens again. But I don't make a habit of falling short on my promises." He runs his finger up my forearm leaving a trail of goosebumps rippling up in his wake.

"Thank you. For the record, the scones are the best I've ever had," I add with a giggle.

He pulls my body into his and wraps his arms around me. I'm overwhelmed with a sense of happiness, calm, and security. I could stay here with him forever.

"I want to be the man who never makes you feel anything but good." His words feel like a promise and we seal them with a sweet kiss.

Epilogue: Cassie, Two Years Later

Patrick and I reconnected at the fundraiser and we haven't parted since. Life by his side is everything I ever wanted and more. When I got pregnant just a few weeks into our relationship, Patrick was thrilled. Being the old-fashioned man he is, he insisted that we get married before our son was born. To be fair, it didn't take a whole lot of convincing. I couldn't wait to be his wife.

We bought a home on the outskirts of Misty Mountain. Patrick made sure there was enough space for our whole family. Now our son Bryan has a room right down the hall from Grandma's suite.

I spend my time baking, cleaning, and taking care of the people I love. It's a beautiful life full of bliss. Today is extra special because it's Bryan's second birthday. Patrick's brothers Taylor and Joshua are here with their wives and our son is enthusiastic about opening his presents in front of his cousins.

Patrick comes to stand by my side, wrapping his arm around my waist. My eyes go glassy as we watch Bryan tear through one package after the next. He squeals with delight each time he uncovers a toy and has to be coaxed into opening the next package.

When there's only one left, Patrick picks up the blue shiny bag and hands it to our son. "Looks like this one is from mommy." Patrick raises an eyebrow in my direction.

I ignore my husband's expectant glance and my stomach flutters with bubbles of excitement as Bryan tears into the bag. When he finds a shirt rolled up at the bottom, Bryan tosses it aside with an adorable grimace of disappointment which draws laughter from the adults in the room.

"Bring it here honey, let's see it," Gram says. She holds her hands out and Bryan runs the shirt over to her.

Gram holds the blue shirt up and shakes it, holding it up for all to see. There's a collective gasp.

"What?" Gram rushes to flip it around.

Patrick repeats the words scrawled across the shirt. "Two more pumpkins coming this fall." Then he turns to me. "You have to be kidding!" Patrick's face twists up into an excited grin and he plants his hand low on my belly.

"They're boys," I whisper, my nose scrunched up in the middle.

"Three Henderson brothers, the next generation..." Patrick stops talking and his eyes go glassy. "I can't wait to meet them."

Our friends and family shower us with cheers of congratulations and warm wishes. I love the life Patrick and I have created together and I can't wait to fall in love with the new additions to our family.

Perfect Pick, Chapter One: Joshua

"**H**ey! Taylor, Patrick," I call out to my brothers from across the pumpkin patch. "There's a... kid." I stop talking because it's pointless, they can't hear me above the loud chug of the tractor working it's way across the field.

When the station asked for us firefighters to volunteer at this three-day fundraiser at the pumpkin patch, I was on board. I've been craving something to add some color to my black and white world. Everyday is the same right now. Clock in, run calls, workout, go home, repeat.

I figured at least here I'd get to bale some hay or drive a tractor and I have done both. I've already used the pumpkin launcher this morning too, which was on par with what I imagined I'd be doing here. But no one told me I'd be watching a crying kid alone.

I wonder how she ended up way out here on the outskirts of the pumpkin patch all alone. She can't be more than four, maybe five and there isn't an adult in sight. I wonder if she stowed away in one of the covered wagons that the tractors tow across the property. She easily could have, they leave them parked all over the patch.

The little girl is adorable with her hair tied into pigtails and bright green eyes. Under normal circumstances, I'd say hello, maybe even offer to buy her some cotton candy. But she's all alone and beside herself which means I am completely out of my element.

I decide to go with what I know. I approach the little bucket of tears the same way I would any person who is crying when I arrive on scene at a fire. I step toward her and extend my hand to her. "Hello, I'm

Joshua. Firefighter with our local Misty Mountain station. I can help you."

She doesn't take my hand. Instead, the teary eyed toddler looks horrified and my assertive tone only seems to exasperate the crying. She covers her face with her hands.

I scramble for another solution. "Oh boy, uh... okay, do you like funny dog videos?"

The little girl temporarily pauses. She leans back against a bale of hay and gives me a slight nod. "I want a dog but my mom says we can't have one because she's too busy."

"Okay, great. Now we're getting somewhere." I fish my phone out of my pocket and wait while it searches for reception.

This is so ironic. I'm literally the least qualified Henderson brother to deal with this. None of us have kids, at least not yet. But Taylor is the oldest and he's always had a parental way about him. Patrick recently dated a woman with a son. They'd know exactly what to do.

I on the other hand have been largely single for almost all my life. Dating whoever. Coming and going as I please, and as a result, never learning what to do when you encounter a little girl with big tears. My phone takes it's time trying to connect to the internet way out here and I turn my head on a swivel looking for a parent. There still isn't anyone to be seen.

"Well, it looks like I can't get online... but if you like dogs, I can show you a picture of a really cool one." This seems to stop her tears immediately and the girl looks at me with renewed interest.

"Okay," her voice shakes and it breaks my heart.

"Cool, take a look at this guy. He's a Dalmatian, that's why he has so many spots. His name is Cinder and he lives at the firehouse. Here he is on the fire engine. There he's wearing a cool hat. He's sharing ice cream with me."

I flip through my photos and the girl's face changes from upset to delighted in a few seconds flat. I swell with relief. Her tears dry up completely when I get to the photos from Cinder's last birthday party and she leans forward to get a closer look at my phone.

"Tomorrow is my birthday. My party is here at the petting zoo. I wanted to come to find the animals to tell them I'll see them tomorrow at my party but now I don't know where the animals are and I don't know where my mom is. I told her I was going to find the animals. She didn't come." The girl puts her hands on her hips and her bottom lip quivers.

"Got it. Well, you're in luck because I can help you find your mom. I bet she's looking for you too. What's your name?"

"My name is Autumn... but how can you help? You don't know what my mom looks like." She raises an eyebrow in suspicion.

"Autumn, I told you, I'm a firefighter, I can do anything. Now let's get you over to the petting zoo." I take a muddy step into the field, but Autumn doesn't follow me.

Instead, I turn to see her squinting her eyes at me in a look somewhere between compliance and stranger danger. I note the return of glassy tears building behind her eyes. "I do want to pet the goats, but I don't know."

"Okay, well I promise if you come with me I will let you pet them. And...hmm, well, do you want to take that tractor to get over to them? I drove it earlier. What do you say?" I step into the tractor and breathe a sigh of relief when I see the keys still in the ignition.

Autumn raises her eyebrows and her face lights up. "Really?"

"Yeah, why not? It's a hay-ride for one. Hop in the back, sit on the hay, and hold on, okay?"

"You know what, you can come to my party tomorrow. You can see all the animals too!" She meets my gaze with a gapped tooth smile.

Just like that, we're buddies. Autumn scrambles up the steps and into the covered wagon. She plants herself on a bale of hay and when I look back at her, she gives me an enthusiastic thumbs up.

I hop into the driver's seat. The tractor coughs, sputters, and then roars to life. As we bounce around the pumpkin patch, Autumn squeals with joy, and I look for a frantic mother in the crowd.

As we get closer to the petting zoo, it doesn't take me long to spot the top of a woman's head surrounded by the pumpkin patch security team. I turn off the tractor and when I do, Autumn calls out to her mother.

The woman with tear-stained cheeks and gorgeous green eyes to match her daughters takes a step toward us. When she does, I'm blown away. I'm overwhelmed with emotion. Goosebumps ripple down my spine. The hair on my arms stands on end. There's something about this stunning woman that makes me think we were meant to meet.

"Autumn, what in the world? What are you doing up there? Get down here right now. You can't wander off like that." She makes her way to the steps of the wagon and when Autumn climbs out, the woman crouches to wrap her arms around her daughter.

"Okay Mom, I was just looking for the animals."

"Your dad will be here in a few minutes, you're heading to his house for the night. I thought you were right next to me. You scared me, honey."

"She's okay, I promise I took good care of her."

My voice seems to startle the woman and she blinks up at me. From this close, she's even more beautiful than I thought. Her skin is tanned and supple. Her body is curvy in all the right places and everything about her draws me in.

Chapter Two: Megan

I'm so focused on my relief over finding my daughter that I almost don't notice the man standing in front of me. But once I look up it's impossible to look away. He's breathtaking.

The man is wearing a blue firefighter shirt with black pants and I assume he's one of the volunteers. He's tall with dark eyes and even darker hair. He's got the kind of chiseled jawline you just don't forget. Silhouetted in the bright light of the afternoon sun, he looks like something out of a dream.

"Thank you for finding her, I'm Megan." I tuck a wild strand of hair behind my ear.

"Joshua Henderson, nice to meet you."

"You too. It's a parent's worst nightmare to lose your kid like that, you know?" I look closely at his worry-free, wrinkle-free, skin and decide that this guy has no idea what I'm talking about. He most definitely does not have children. In fact, he looks pretty young himself.

"I bet. But it was no problem, she and I were just hanging out. I hear she has a big birthday party planned tomorrow and that she wants a dog." He lets out a chuckle and his smile reveals a shallow dimple on one side of his face. "Come on, get her a dog."

"Well, maybe one day when Mom isn't working so many shifts at the hospital. I'm a nurse and between her weekends at her dad's house and my own hectic schedule, it'd hardly be fair to the pup. But I'm not surprised she tried to plead her case." I glance down at my daughter and she bats her eyes with mock innocence. "Anyway, we should be heading out. Her father will be here soon." I turn to leave, Autumn tucked against my side.

"Actually, I can't let you go yet. You see, I promised Autumn that if she came with me, I'd let her pet the goats." Joshua reaches out and wraps his hand around my wrist. The simple gesture sends a zap of electricity whipping through me and leaves a trail of goosebumps rippling across my skin in its wake.

"What?" I look up at him and his dark eyes burn into mine.

"I keep my promises and I did make a promise. It'll just take five minutes. Shall we?" Joshua flashes a dashing smile in my direction then holds out his elbow to me.

For a moment, I'm in so much shock that I can hardly speak. This is straight from the pages of one of my romance novels, not something that happens in real life. Especially not to people like me, yet here I am.

"Sure. Yes, let's go see the goats. Quickly." I ignore the offer of his elbow and wrap my hand tightly around Autumn's.

"Yay!" Autumn squeals with excitement.

As we follow Joshua across the muddy pumpkin patch my mind whirls. Everything about this day is unexpected. I thought I was just going to quickly make a stop at this fundraiser that is benefitting the hospital where I work. I thought I'd show my face, drop Autumn with her father, and be on my way to get ready for her party.

I didn't think I'd lose my five-year-old in the crowd of people. I never expected she'd be rescued by this bag of muscles. And I absolutely did not think I'd be walking behind him as we take my kid to look at the goats together.

Joshua is chivalrous. And hot. And good with kids. But none of that matters because I promised myself that I would not get into another relationship, at least not anytime soon. Not until my daughter is older. Not until I become a better picker of men.

Autumn deserves a quality man in her life as much as I do, but having her witness the bad ones coming and going isn't good for a kid.

My ex-husband is already parading a never-ending list of girlfriends in front of her. He can do whatever he wants, but I made a commitment to myself and to my daughter that I would not put her through a revolving door of men.

"Here we go." Joshua pushes the gate and holds it open as Autumn and I step inside.

He puts a quarter in the machine and turns the crank until a handful of feed spits out of the bottom. When he pours it into Autumn's hands she squeals with excitement and takes off toward the goat pen. Then he pulls another quarter out of his pocket and gets a second scoop of pellets.

"Megan, hold your hands out, you're going to feed them too."

"No." I step away from him in surprise. "I don't do goat feeding. Farm life isn't really my thing but I'm happy Autumn gets to have the experience."

Joshua lets out a hearty chuckle. "You must be mistaken, it wasn't a question. This is yours, come on now."

Before I can object again, Joshua is taking my hands in his and I'm giggling like a teenager as he pours the goat feed into my palms. He places a hand on my lower back and steers me toward the pen.

"Mom! You're doing it too?" Autumn claps her hands when she sees me and hops up and down. "Be brave! It feels so ticklish."

I hold my hands near the gate and let out a yelp when the goat's tongue presses against the inside of my palms. Joshua wraps his steadying arms around me with a laugh. It feels good to be tucked up against his washboard abs and rock-solid chest. Heat bubbles between us. I don't know what's come over me, but all of a sudden, I don't want to move.

I watch the goats frolic and climb through their pen. I'm lost in the feeling of being this close to the handsome stranger behind me when one of the goats falls on his side. He doesn't get up. In fact, he doesn't move at all. I stiffen and my eyes widen in horror.

I gasp. "Oh my gosh, is that one dead? Did he just die? My kid just saw a goat die..." I slap a hand over my mouth.

Joshua bursts into laughter. "No, you've never heard of a fainting goat? Also, aren't you a nurse? Shouldn't you be climbing the fence to revive him if that was the case?"

I can't help but join in the fun. Joshua and I laugh until our cheeks hurt. He brings out a playful side of me that has been gone for far too long. He doesn't stop teasing me until Autumn appears between us. She turns her head from me to Joshua, her eyes cutting the small space between us and it snaps me back to reality.

I clear my throat. "Okay, Joshua, thanks again. We really should be going, I'll bet Autumn's dad is already in the parking lot. Come on, Autumn."

"Can I go look at the chickens on the way out?" Autumn begs.

"Sure," I tell her.

As Autumn scampers off in front of us, Joshua turns to me. The dashing smile is prominently back on his face. "I have an idea. You are going to walk your daughter to the car, drop her off with her dad, and then meet me right back here. I think you need a little taste of farm life. So I'm making you mine for the next couple hours."

"Why do you keep saying questions as if they are facts?" I tease him but the rich, deep, tone in his voice makes it impossible for me to want to say no. But, still, it's crazy... isn't it? "It's tempting, but I really should be headed home. I hadn't planned on staying."

"I hadn't planned on meeting you, but damn am I glad I did. Right-back here as soon as you drop her off. I'm going to take you on a hayride, we'll launch a few pumpkins, and you'll tell me a little more about yourself. That's all I want. You'll still be home in plenty of time for whatever it is you have planned, I promise I'll take care of you." He grabs my hand and gives it a gentle squeeze that sends another round of shock waves pulsating through me.

Of all the things he could have said, why did it have to be that he will take care of me? That one simple sentence is what I've ached to hear for years. I never heard it from my ex-husband, not even from my own parents. So when it comes out of his mouth, it melts me.

"You drive a hard bargain," I smirk at him and push back the part of my mind that wonders what else he might drive hard.

"Then it's a date." Joshua winks at me.

"No, it's not."

Autumn and I walk hand in hand toward the car. As soon as I'm away from Joshua, my senses return. What am I thinking? Who goes around picking up women at pumpkin patches? What kind of mom am I to ignore my plans to prepare Autumn's party to go on a hayride with a random, smoldering dude?

"Mom," Autumn tugs on my arm. "Do you like Joshua?"

"What? No. I mean, he's fine. I don't even know him." I always forget how perceptive my daughter can be. Then I can't help but add, "Do you like him?"

"Yes, he's so nice! And he makes you smile a lot."

My cheeks flush with warmth. "Okay, that's enough, there's your dad, see his truck?" I point in the direction of the parking lot, desperate to change the subject.

AN HOUR LATER, JOSHUA is whipping me around the pumpkin patch on his arm and I am completely lost in him. As I suspected, Joshua is thirty one which means I have a solid five years on him, not to mention a divorce and a daughter. But what he lacks in age, he makes up for with charm.

As we walk, he keeps a firm grasp on me and I like the way it feels. He asks me questions that are too personal for someone I only just met and to my surprise, I answer them with complete honesty. In an even bigger surprise, he really listens.

By his side, I feel heard and safe. I feel beautiful and most of all, I feel like myself. Not the hardened me that has developed in these last few difficult years of separation and divorce, but the real me who I thought I lost so long ago.

Joshua turns to me, a smirk resting on his lips. "Ready? We're headed through the mud. Can you handle it?"

"I can handle it. But where are you taking me?"

"Straight out that way." Joshua points across the pumpkin patch to the cornfield in the distance. "Will you go with me way over there? I think that thing probably has keys in it and I promised you a hayride."

I follow his gaze until my eyes land on a tractor with a covered wagon behind it in the distance. It's washed in the golden sunlight of the setting sun and I can't help but think to myself that everything Joshua touches turns to gold.

"Right now I'd go anywhere with you."

I look up at Joshua and he catches my chin with his hand. My breath quickens as he leans in toward me. My heart races out of control. He holds me with the confidence of a man ten years his senior and the enthusiasm of a teenager with his first love.

Joshua's stare is intoxicating and we're so close, I can feel the heat of his breath on my face. He moves a hand to the back of my head and when his mouth meets mine, there isn't anything soft about it. He devours me.

Tongue parting my lips and stealing my breath. Hands tugging my hair and roaming my curves. It's fireworks and lightning. It's all-encompassing. Earth-shattering. The kind of kiss that changes everything.

By the time he pulls away, my knees are so weak, I fear I might fall over.

Chapter Three: Joshua

By the time we make it out to the tractor, I can't keep my mind on anything other than the intensity of our kiss. The way her breasts felt pressed against my chest. The way I need to make her mine.

I climb onto the tractor and find the keys tucked underneath the driver's seat. But before I can start the engine, Megan straddles me on the front seat of the tractor. Her eyes burn into mine and my body screams for more. I run my hands down the length of her back, breathing into her hair and taking in her tantalizing scent. There's something so sexy about a woman who knows what she wants.

Being this close to her lets me take in all of the details that make her perfect. The roundness in her cheeks. The way her eyes glitter in the setting sun. The swell of her mouth-watering cleavage.

Megan leans in toward me until our lips are almost touching until I can feel the warmth of her breath on my face. I feel her movement in every single part of my body. When I can't stand it for another minute, I plant my mouth on her full pink lips.

The sexual tension between us erupts into a single kiss that makes my heart race and my palms sweat. After that, I'm ignited. Megan melts into my arms and I part her lips with my tongue. My hands roam across every inch of her skin and she's all I can see.

I wrap my hands around her waist and pull her into me. The weight of her body on my lap as she rocks against me makes my dick twitch firm against the zipper of my pants. I thrust my hips up, grinding myself against her, and trail kisses across her ear.

When she wraps her hands around my neck, I press my face into her chest. Her perky nipples beg to be teased beneath her shirt. I run my hands across her mounds and roll her tight nipples between my fingers before slipping one into my mouth. I suckle at her buds and heat builds low in my stomach. Megan moans for more.

I've never wanted anyone more than I want Megan right now. She's set off a whirlwind of lust in me. I'm drowning in her and I don't want to come up for air.

She leans away from me. "Come on." Megan's mouth pulls into a smirk as she climbs off my lap, pulling me behind her.

We make our way into the covered wagon behind the tractor. Megan lays on her back between the hay bales, pulling me down with her. She lets out a giggle as I pull her pants down and then move over the top of her.

My eyes linger on her as I try to control my hunger for her skin on mine. The sensual curves of her body and the outline of her breasts against my chest don't help the situation. Megan leans into my touch as I run my fingers across every part of her freshly exposed skin, leaving a trail of goosebumps rippling up in my wake.

Megan's hands are under my shirt, roaming my chest. Her fingernails drag down my sides. She tugs at my pants and makes quick work of unbuttoning them. By the time my throbbing, firm, length springs free, my tip is already glistening with desire for her.

She reaches for my member and there's nothing I want more than for her to put it in her mouth. But I promised I'd take care of her and that applies to the bedroom... and the covered wagon too, so I inch my way down her body.

I press on the inside of her thighs and she lets them fall open for me. I keep going until I reach the sweet spot between her legs. I use my tongue to brush against her hot, swollen nub and Megan rolls her hips against my face. The taste of her on my tongue makes me hungry for more.

From there it's a blur. I'm lost in a frenzy of licking, sucking, and plunging inside her with my tongue. Megan's thighs quiver and tense, her breathing becomes erratic. She exhales moans that fill the wagon and I slap a firm hand over her mouth.

I hold her there, exhaling my name through clenched teeth, hands grasping at the hay underneath her. I work on her until she's begging for more. Until the anticipation of her velvety tightness makes me pulsate.

When I finally position myself on top of her, I can already tell she's drenched. I line myself up between her open thighs and thrust inside with one mighty push. I grunt, frantic to keep hold of myself as I feel her walls stretch to accommodate my girth.

She rocks her hips in time with my thrusts and it spurs me on. I cling to her tits and lower my chest closer to hers as I pound her into the hay. Her body fits mine with incredible precision. We move in perfect tandem until two become one. Megan is all I can see.

Then Megan's body is racked with tense tremors. When I put my hand back over her mouth, she sucks on my finger and it threatens to send me over the edge. I wrap my other hand in her hair and hold on until her walls collapse on me.

Finally, Megan lets out a moan of release, and her body contracts as she rides a wave of orgasm. Watching her release pushes me over the edge too, I can't help but let go. I explode deep inside of her and Megan milks me to the last drop.

When it's over and we're drenched in sweat, I wrap my arms around her from behind. Megan leans her head back against my chest. I just took her body and claimed it as my own, but it isn't enough. I want to spend all night every night entangled with her. I want to ravage her again, I don't think it would ever be enough. But I settle for planting a kiss on the top of her head and tightening my grip on her as she relaxes into me.

Chapter Four: Megan

A half-hour after Joshua helps me back into my pants, he and I are making our way out of the cornfield hand in hand. But I could have laid in the back of that tractor nestled into his side all night.

He has to be the most charming man I've ever met. He's thoughtful and sincere, everything I've ever wanted really. It's too bad he's so young. He'll forever stay in my mind as that one, perfect, date.

"That was a lot of fun." Joshua's words are a throaty growl.

"Agreed, I hate to see it end." I commit to memory the warmth of his arm wrapped around my waist.

"Same. So let's not end it. Let's keep this going. Let me take you out for a late dinner." Joshua's dark eyes reflect the moonlight.

All I want to do is say yes to him, to get lost in him all over again. But I'm a mom of a little girl who is expecting a fabulous birthday party tomorrow. So I push all those emotions back. "You're sweet, but I need to head home. I have so many details to tie up for Autumn's big day tomorrow."

"Aww, you're breaking my heart. In fact, that's the worst news I've heard all day. At least let me walk you to your car." Joshua squeezes my hip and pulls my body into his. His touch sends warmth bubbling through me. "But I'll see you tomorrow at the big birthday bash so waiting just one night won't be too bad."

I freeze and my chest tightens. "Wait... what?"

"The big party tomorrow, here at the pumpkin patch. Autumn told me all about it so I figured I'd come and bring a big present. You know,

I want to win her over because I kind of like her mom." Joshua flashes me a brilliant, dazzling smile and I stiffen.

I blink and my head swirls with confusion. I like Joshua too but I hardly know him. "That's really sweet, but I don't go around introducing my daughter to every guy I meet. It isn't good for kids to have adults in and out of their lives like that."

"What do you mean? She and I are practically old friends at this point," he lets out a light-hearted chuckle. "Besides, who said anything about in and out? I'm all in with you."

I swallow the lump in my throat and take a step backward. I'm so confused. If it were really *just* me, I'd be all in with him too. But that isn't how my life works. I'm a mom first, even when it's hard. "I don't think it's a good idea. I'm sorry but you aren't invited."

Lines crease Joshua's forehead. He looks stunned and I feel terrible.

"Wow, I uh, I guess I read this whole situation wrong. My mistake." He rubs the back of his neck. "Well, that's all right. We'll have a lot of time to get to know each other. Maybe I'll buy her a Christmas gift instead."

My stomach clenches. I know he thinks he's telling the truth. In fact, I wish that things would play out like that, but I've been let down too many times. The truth is he'll probably be long gone by Thanksgiving. Once the realities of having a child set in, things change, guys don't stick around.

"Listen, today was so much fun, but it's probably for the best. You don't want to be tied down to the routine of a toddler. Being with someone who has a kid isn't that much fun, I get it. There aren't any hard feelings." I keep my voice steady as I tell my lie. "We live in two different worlds."

"Hey, come on. I know we only just met and it sounds crazy, but there's something here between us. I can feel it. I know I'm not wrong about this." He crosses his arms over his chest. "I think you feel it too. Why are you pushing me away?"

"Ah, my life doesn't work like that. It's not as simple as deciding whether or not I feel something. Not for me, not as a mom." Hot tears build behind my eyes. I'm flustered, my words jumble in my mind.

"Okay, don't worry, I won't show up at your party. I'm not over here thinking of ways I can create more problems in your life. But I won't pretend I think you're making the right decision either because I know you're not." There isn't any bite to Joshua's words, only hurt.

WHEN I STEP INTO MY quiet house, I get to work on the favor bags for Autumn's party. I fill the balloons with helium and finish frosting the cupcakes. But my mind only stays focused on one thing, Joshua.

Today was a whirlwind of emotions. It was something from a movie. The man literally swept me off my feet. Only, he chose the wrong girl. He is a hero from any romance novel, a handsome firefighter with a heart of gold, but I'm not a heroine. I'm a mom who has introduced her daughter to one too many boyfriends who didn't care about her and I'm determined not to do it again.

My losses shouldn't be hers. I owe it to her to keep her life as stable as I can. But at the same time, I feel terrible for dismissing Joshua like that. There is something about him that makes me hope he is the right person for me, but how can I be sure? I've trusted the wrong people before.

By the time I go to bed, one thing is for certain, I owe him an apology at the very least.

Chapter Five: Joshua

"What's wrong with you?" My brother Taylor loads up the launcher with a small pumpkin and lets it fly.

"Just one day of farm life has you wishing you were back at the station, huh?" Patrick adds with a chuckle.

"Ha. No, farm life I can handle. It's women I can't figure out." I blow out a frustrated breath. "I hardly slept last night."

Taylor turns on a dime and heads back toward me, letting his pumpkin fall to the ground. "What woman? Mom?"

"Very funny. No. Megan, the mom of the kid I found yesterday. I ended up making a night of it with her and it was... different than what I expected. She's incredible, smart, funny, hot as fuck."

"Oh shoot," Patrick laughs.

"But?" Taylor raises his eyebrows expectantly.

"But I thought everything was going well and out of nowhere, she freaked out. I assumed I was going to her kid's birthday party this afternoon. I mean, it's here at the pumpkin patch and I'll be here anyway. But Megan doesn't want me to go... and that's fine I guess, but it's like she doesn't trust that I'm taking this thing between us seriously."

Taylor cringes and shifts his eyes to the ground. "Oh, man."

"Yikes." Patrick lets a chuckle escape into the brisk air.

I roll my eyes at the two of them. "Fine, let's hear it. I assume I'm in the wrong but you can tell me why." Not that my brothers have ever needed an invitation to tell me when I've missed something.

"She's just worried about her kid," Patrick says. "You're a stranger. You've known her for a day. An adult male who is desperate to go to a six-year-old's birthday party. Dude, that's how people go to jail." Patrick lets out a laugh and after a moment of tense silence, Taylor and I can't help but join in.

"Okay well, when you put it like that I sound creepy." I stretch the tight muscles in my neck. "I may have come on a little strong, but I want to know every part of her. Be in her life for good."

"Then that's what you need to tell her," Taylor says.

An hour of head nods and eye rolls later, it's clear what needs to be done. I thank my brothers for their not-so-subtle suggestion that I may have totally messed this up and excuse myself from my volunteer status for a few hours. I head out to the fire station. I've got to move fast if I'm going to be back here in time.

BY EARLY AFTERNOON, I'm back at the pumpkin patch. Only now, I've got my secret weapon with me. Cinder, our station's fire dog prances off-leash beside me. He's well trained in community events and ready to help me charm my way back into Megan's life.

I set my sights on the petting zoo across the field. The gates are closed and as Cinder and I get closer I can read the handwritten sign.

Reserved for a Private Party.

I exhale and shake my nerves out of my hands. "Come on Cinder, we need to do this quickly before the guests arrive. I don't want to end up in jail for crashing a party."

Cinder looks up at me with knowing eyes and follows me toward the entrance. When I push the gate open, it makes a loud creaking sound and I step inside. Megan is standing on a table hanging a banner. She turns to look at me, then her eyes dart Cinder and back.

"Hi, this is a surprise." Megan's words are soft, but not unkind.

"I'm not here to stay. I'm here to apologize and to help you solve a problem. I know Autumn wants a dog and I know you don't have time for one right now. This is Cinder. He's on loan from the station. I won't stay, but he can... if you want him to. I thought he'd be able to make Autumn smile."

Megan's furrowed eyebrows straighten and her downturned mouth pulls up just a hint, but it's enough for me. I know I'll have to learn to slow things down if I want to stay in her world, and I desperately want to stay.

"Really? That is so thoughtful." She gets closer to us and drops to her knees. "He is pretty cute, you have me there. Hey Cinder, you're just adorable aren't you."

As I watch Megan with Cinder, I'm overwhelmed with the same sensation I felt the very first time I saw her. This woman is supposed to be mine. I know I'm not wrong about us. Now I just have to convince her.

Megan gets to her feet. "Thank you, Autumn will love it. I'm glad you stopped by. I've been up all night wanting to tell you how sorry I am for the way I acted yesterday. You've been nothing but sweet to me and you didn't deserve that. I overreacted. It's just that Autumn is my whole world and most people don't understand that parenting isn't just fun. It's hard and it's selfless a lot of the time." She chews her bottom lip adorably.

"Well, it's a good thing I'm not most people." I pull her toward me and brush a strand of hair away from her face. "Listen, you aren't wrong. I don't have kids and I've never been married, so I don't know what it's like. But I've watched my brothers go through divorces and it left them gutted. It isn't something I ever want to do. So I need you to understand that when I say I'm in this with you, I mean it. I have no reason to commit other than you are the most incredible person I've ever met and you come with this awesome, bonus gift of this brilliant little girl. I want to be a part of your world for the long run when you're ready for it. You don't have to commit to that now, all you need to do is tell me that I can see you again."

I put it all out there. The words hang heavy between us as I try to read the expression on her face. For a long while, she's unreadable. Blinking. Lost in thought. But I breathe a sigh of relief when her mouth turns up at the corners.

"You can see me again. I'd like for you to see me again."

"That's good news. That is such good news." I plant a sweet kiss on the top of her head. My heart leaps in my chest and an enormous grin stretches across my face. "What are you doing after the party?"

"Probably you," she raises one eyebrow and her mouth pulls into a sexy smirk.

Epilogue: Joshua, One Year Later

I started proposing to Megan just one week after our first night together. Naturally, as a mother, she didn't want to rush into anything. I respected that, but it didn't stop me from continuing to ask. Each time she turned me down I smiled because I already knew I was one *no* closer to a *yes*.

Eventually, I did get a yes. It was the happiest day of my life. I told Megan that I would make sure she got the wedding of her dreams. When she told me her dream was the three of us standing in front of our friends and family at the Brew by Brewer pumpkin patch, I was all in. It seemed only fitting that we get married in the same place our relationship started.

Now I stand at the end of the aisle lined with white pumpkins, my heart pounding in my chest. When the music starts, I almost forget to breathe. My brothers Patrick and Taylor give me encouraging pats on the back and I shake my nerves out of my hands.

Autumn makes the world's most adorable flower girl. As she heads toward me, an enormous smile on her face, I can't help but think that everything in my life has been getting me ready to be her father. When she gets to the end of the aisle, I hold out my arms to her and she falls into them. As I wrap her in a tight hug, I admit to myself that I didn't know I was capable of loving someone so fiercely. But I do. There isn't anything I won't do for this sweet little girl.

But as ready as I am for this day to finally be here, nothing could have prepared me for the moment Megan steps out into the pumpkin patch in her lace gown. She's absolutely breathtaking. The dress hugs her curves in all the right spots. The cool fall air makes her veil dance in the wind.

We lock eyes as she starts her walk down the aisle and I can't help the tears that stream down my cheek. Megan is more than I deserve, beautiful, courageous, and thoughtful. Simply put, she's the woman of my dreams.

When she reaches me, I take her hands in mine and look into the eyes that hold my future. I never thought life could be this good. Megan and Autumn are my entire universe and I'm so grateful for all the color they've brought to the drab places in my world.

During the ceremony, I make vows to Kaylee and to Autumn too. I promise to love and protect them with my whole heart for my whole life. In return, Kaylee promises that she will partner with me, lean on me, and trust me with her heart and her daughter.

Looking into Megan's eyes, I see everything I never knew I needed. She's my best friend, my favorite person, and the love of my life. I'm so lucky she chose me to be the man by her side. I can't wait to fall in love every day with this perfect pick of a wife.

Just like that, the officiant pronounces us Mr. and Mrs. Henderson. We seal our vows with a kiss that sends whoops and cheers rippling through the crowd. Megan and I walk hand in hand into our happily ever after.

HEY READER,

I'm so happy you're here! Doesn't Brew by Brewer seem like the place to be for Halloween? I know a couple who thought it'd be perfect. So perfect they planned a spooky wedding there... Let's just say things didn't go exactly as they had planned. Keep reading for a sneak peek at Holdays at Brew by Brewer. Go ahead, fall in love. You deserve it!

Xoxo, Elsie

HOLIDAYS AT BREW BY Brewer, Spooked
Chapter One: Shawn

It's like my body knew the moment I stepped onto Misty Mountain soil and it went into high alert. I've only been back here a few hours and my stomach is wound into tight knots. My hands are clammy, the muscles in my throat are perpetually clenched. I suppose it's some kind of muscle-memory-trauma-response. In fact, I'm sure of it.

My little sister Stella is literally the only person in the world who could get me back to Misty Mountain after all that's happened. Not that I'm ever too far from it no matter how far I go, this town hangs over me like a shadow even when I'm at home in the city.

There's a constant reel of memories that play in my mind on a loop. Normally I can keep them at bay, but the way they come to life against the backdrop of my small hometown is downright spooky.

"Sir, are you checking in?" The woman behind the counter at the hotel at Brew by Brewer looks up at me. "Sir, your name please."

I snap my attention back to her. "Sorry, it's Shawn Willman. I have two adjoining rooms booked, please."

"Not a problem, I'll need to see some identification and the card you used to make the reservation. Also, will your guest need a key?"

I hesitate. "Yeah, I suppose she will." I take a step away from the counter and then lean back in. "You know what, why don't you leave her key here and she can pick it up when she arrives. Please hold it for Kaylee Allen."

Saying her name aloud for the first time feels odd and unnatural. I look at the woman's face to see if she registered anything out of the ordinary in my tone. But she hardly looks up from her keyboard at all.

"Sure thing. Give me a moment and I'll have that all squared away for you." The woman disappears behind the counter.

I look around and take in the sights of the hotel. They've done an impressive job getting this place ready for Halloween. Not that it needed a ton of work. The Brewer family has converted the ancient poor farm in our town into a luxury resort, but they've kept all its original, old-world, charm.

Now, ancient chandeliers, old oak carved doors, and brass fixtures are topped with faux spider webs. A man dressed as a werewolf walks casually through the lobby. Leave it to my little sister to hold a wedding that lasts not one but three days and ends on Halloween.

It isn't usually a romantic holiday. But in Stella's case, the dude she's marrying, Spencer Brewer, is pretty sinister, so I guess it makes sense.

Spencer Brewer has been an unwelcome part of my life for the last six years since he knocked my sister up. I'll give it to the guy, he made a cute kid, my niece is to die for. But that's the only thing he has going for him as far as I can tell.

Well, that and the fact that his family isn't too bad either. I went to school with the Brewers who live here in Misty Mountain, and they're all right, nothing like their cousin Spencer. They own this property and offered it up free of charge for the ceremony.

"Uncle Shawn!" The voice of my adorable niece McKenna sounds behind me and I turn to see her running toward me, arms open, and a gapped tooth smile on her face.

"Kenna," my heart skips a beat.

When I see her, all is right in my world, if only for a minute. When I scoop down and pick her up, I feel full again. McKenna seems to be the only thing that fills the gaping hole inside me.

McKenna and I have been video chatting on our usual schedule, but I feel a pang of sadness stab at my stomach when I realize she's so much bigger than the last time I saw her. "I think you grew a whole foot. What are you, like twenty-five now?"

"Uncle Shawn, I'm still six," she giggles and I put her down.

"If it isn't my big brother, it's good to see you." My sister Stella hugs me.

She of all people understands what it's costing me to be back here for the weekend. I can't help but think of how many times she's come through for me in the last five years and I feel a pang of guilt stab at me for living so far away.

"It's the bride herself, how are you doing with all of this? They certainly did good by your spooky wedding theme. Which is fitting given you're marrying Spencer." I lower my voice and lean in toward my sister, staying out of my niece's earshot. "Are you sure you want to go through with this?" I know I shouldn't ask but I'm the only person who can get away with it.

"Stop it," Stella shakes her head at me. "I'm already in the situation, all you can do now is support me. Besides, a Halloween-themed wedding is worth it if only to see my big brother in an array of costumes... and to hang out with your mysterious new girlfriend. I literally can't wait to meet her!"

Me neither. I wonder what she'll be like. I wonder if I can pull this off.

"She, uh... Kaylee had to fly in late. She had a work thing. But she'll be here." I swallow back my nerves.

McKenna hops up and down, her dark hair in pigtails. "I've got so many costumes! I have a princess one, a zombie, and..." McKenna covers her mouth to control her fits of giggles. "And Uncle Shawn you aren't going to guess... a cat costume! With a tail!"

"That is so cool, I can't wait to see them," I tell her.

As I chat with my sister and niece I have to admit that being in Misty Mountain feels better than I thought it would. I'd forgotten about the small-town charm. The way people say hello to you when they pass. The simple luxury of inhaling clean, mountain air and the way my niece lights up when I talk to her.

"What's up, Big Will?" Spencer's voice is like nails on a chalkboard and it punctures my moment of bliss. Spencer talks four decibels above everyone else in the lobby. He stands uncomfortably close to me and claps me on the back with unnecessary force. His white-blond hair is thinner than the last time I saw him, and his eyebrows are nonexistent.

"Hello, Spencer. Just a reminder that literally no one calls me that." I try to keep my face from pinching into tight lines. I glance at my sister and for her sake, I muster up as much good-willed enthusiasm as I can. "Congratulations."

Spencer's mouth turns down at the corners. "I figured it was time I made it official with the old ball and chain. I mean, I already put a baby in her, I'm already stuck. Plus she's got a decent job for now, so if she wants to be a sugar momma for life, I'm here for it."

Good-willed enthusiasm, over. All I can think to respond with is *you son of a bitch*. But I look at my niece McKenna and keep myself together. "Come on now, I'm sure you're looking forward to making your family official."

But Spencer is already engrossed in some kind of video on his phone, so much so that he doesn't even seem to hear me. So much so, that when my niece reaches for her dad's hand, he doesn't flinch except to pull it away.

"Spencer." My tone is a thinly veiled threat.

He chuckles. "It's cats with bread on their heads, paired with women with big tits... Classic." Spencer holds up the video in my direction. "Hey man, I'm gonna ditch these broads in a bit and get drunk to get through this weekend. You down?"

"Absolutely not. Unbelievable." I turn my head away from him, fury bubbling in my stomach. My eyes flick to Stella, but she's avoiding my stare. I know my sister well enough to say with confidence that it isn't an accident, but I lean in toward her anyway. "You're okay with this? You're voluntarily marrying... this?"

But Stella only rolls her eyes with a shrug and waves me off as McKenna rattles on excitedly about her costumes. For being one of the smartest people I know, Stella isn't making good choices right now and it makes me sick.

My list of grievances with Spencer is long and detailed. But all of them start and end with the way he disrespects my sister and takes my niece for granted. The woman behind the desk finally returns with my room key and I breathe out with relief. At least I have the option of taking myself out of the situation before I say something I'll regret.

"Here you are, we'll leave this key for your guest. Give us a call at the front desk if you need anything." The woman hands over my room key along with a map of the seventy-four-acre property.

"Thanks." I turn to my sister. "I'm gonna head up to my room."

"Okay, don't forget, the rehearsal dinner is tonight. It's full costume required and it'll be so much fun. I know Mom and Dad are more than ready to see you. Our wedding planner Lauren has pulled out all the stops. This weekend should be downright scary," Stella says.

My eyes flash to Spencer. "Now that I can believe. Kenna, come here girl, give Uncle Shawn a hug. I can't wait to see your cool costume in a little bit."

"Later Big Will," Spencer calls over his shoulder without bothering to look up from his phone.

I all but fly up the stairs to my room, more than ready to put some space between Spencer and me. As hard as I try, I can't see what my sister sees in that guy. Her choosing him is not something I'll ever understand.

When I step inside my hotel room, I'm relieved to see that there is in fact an adjoining door. It's an essential piece to the puzzle of this wedding weekend. The last thing I want to do is make her uncomfortable. I crack it open and step through into what will be Kaylee's room. It's weird to think that at any moment, Kaylee Allen, who has been nothing more than a name on a piece of paper, will be here in person.

My assistant helped me come up with three couples' costumes for this weekend. She's packaged each into its own bag with all the parts and labeled them for me. Best of all, she didn't ask any questions, she's good like that. She's more than happy to give me my space and I dread the day she retires.

I find the three bags with Kaylee's name on them and lay them on her bed. Then I step out and close the adjoining door. I plop onto my own bed and attempt to fire through some work emails. But it isn't any use, I can't focus. Rather, I can't believe this is what I've been reduced to, hiring a date for my sister's wedding.

It's odd, but I couldn't see any other options. So I was as careful with the selection process as possible. I needed someone who could meet all of my specifications. It'd be nice if she was friendly, or at least not unpleasant. It'd be even better if she was attractive, but I thought I might be pushing my luck.

The list of things I'd prefer stretched on and on. But when it came down to writing the advertisement, I could only think of five things that actually mattered.

Needed: Wedding Date/ Fake Girlfriend

1. *No husband or boyfriend. Please no jealous psychos showing up.*
2. *No kids. In my experience, adding a child to anything makes it immediately complicated.*
3. *No breaking character. We need to look like a couple madly in love for the duration of the three-day event. Must cling to our agreed-upon backstory.*
4. *Couples costumes are required for events, I will provide them.*
5. *No sex or intimacy of any kind required. I'm not a creep.*

When I saw it in black and white, it seemed like a lot to ask, so I made sure to offer an astronomical amount of cash. It only made sense to exchange something I have too much of for something I don't have at all... and it worked.

I received hundreds of replies. Immediately I went to work, weeding out the spam and having my assistant help pair down the pile. When I found Kaylee's application, something in her simple, kind responses drew me to her. She seemed down to earth. Normal. Drama-free. It was a process to find her, but it was better than the alternative of showing up back in Misty Mountain alone.

It was worth the effort to avoid the pitying looks and questions. Everyone thinks they know how long you should grieve. But this, what I'm doing, isn't grief, I'm past that. This is an acknowledgment of the fact that I am meant to be alone.

I tried love once, and it was a supreme effort that took me to hell and back. In the end, it wasn't meant to be. I've made my peace with that, but it seems no one else has. Ever since it happened, my parents worry about me. My sister worries about me. My old friends worry, but I don't. I'm okay on my own.

As the afternoon winds on, my nerves start to get the better of me. Kaylee and I have emailed back and forth, but it's been all business. It'd be nice to at least meet this woman for more than five minutes before we have to convince people that we are desperately in love.

I wonder if she's here yet. I don't hear anything next door. I look at the clock and bide my time, taking a shower, and unzipping the bag labeled, *Shawn Outfit #1*. On top of the outfit, there's a note in my assistant's old-lady penmanship.

Sorry, this is all they had last minute. The other two are better. Enjoy, Margie

When I peer inside, at first I have no idea what I'm even looking at. It looks like some kind of blue suit made from plastic. It's complete with a white button-down shirt, pink suspenders, and a matching pink bowtie. It isn't until I pull out the plastic wig that I realize my lovely assistant has made me a Ken doll. I chuckle to myself as I pull it on. As if this day isn't weird enough, I might as well be the least sexy man in America.

When the clock hits four, I only have an hour until my sister's rehearsal dinner and I pull out my phone and punch in a text to Kaylee.

Me: *Hello, This is Shawn Willman. I'd like to meet if you are up for it.*

Before she can respond, my stomach bubbles and anxiety rises in my throat. I punch out another text.

Me: *Although of course you aren't required to spend any additional time with me per our contract, so if you are not interested that's okay too.*

I am completely off my game. My divorce was five years ago at this point and admittedly, I haven't dated much since then, but I didn't think I was this bad. Three minutes pass and I start to worry whether she's come at all. Shaking my head at myself, I punch out a third message.

Me: *I will be outside of your door when it's time to go per our agreement.*

Nerves prickle on the back of my neck. What if I've completely misread the situation? What if she's miserable or if our connection is totally unrealistic? If my family sees right through this, then all the groundwork I've laid to convince them that I've gotten over the sadness in my past will be for nothing.

Tap. Tap.

When I hear a soft knock coming from the other side of the room, I take a step toward the front door. With this many Willman's running around the Brewer property this weekend, I can't just be opening the door for anyone. Lest I find myself in a three-hour conversation with my aunt who lives with her cats.

But when I look out of the peephole, there isn't anyone to be found. Then I hear the soft tapping again and turn on a dime when I realize the knocking is coming from the adjoining door.

Read Holidays at Brew by Brewer available in paperback and on Kindle Unlimited!

Dear reader, can we keep in touch? There's so many more mountain men waiting to steal your heart and I want to make sure you don't miss a single minute. Use the QR code at the end of this book to subscribe to my newsletter. Hope to see you there! Xoxo, Elsie

About the Author

Elsie James is proud to be a lifelong curvy girl. She writes stories about beautiful, strong, women who always find their happily ever afters. Her books are romantic, sweet, and steamy with a whole lot of heart.

CONNECT WITH ELSIE

Facebook: @authorelsiejames [1]

Instagram: @authorelsiejames[2]

TikTok: @elsiejamesauthor [3]

Amazon: amazon.com/author/elsiejames[4]

Email: elsiejames@authorelsiejames.com

Join my Newsletter to receive a FREE book: https://BookHip.com/RZSKJF[5]

---

1.   https://www.facebook.com/authorelsiejames/

2.   https://www.instagram.com/authorelsiejames/

3.   https://www.tiktok.com/@elsiejamesauthor

4.   http://amazon.com/author/elsiejames

5.   https://bookhip.com/RZSKJF